Liberty

BY DARCY PATTISON

Mims House
Little Rock, AR

Mims House
1309 Broadway
Little Rock, AR 72202, USA
www.mimshouse.com

Publisher's Note: This is a work of fiction. Names, characters, places, and incidents are a product of the author's imagination. Locales and public names are sometimes used for atmospheric purposes. Any resemblance to actual people, living or dead, or to businesses, companies, events, institutions, or locales is completely coincidental.

Publisher's Cataloging-in-Publication data

Names: Pattison, Darcy.
Title: Liberty / by Darcy Pattison.
Description: Little Rock [Arkansas]: Mim's House, 2016.
Identifiers: ISBN 978-1-62944-064-4 (Hardcover) | ISBN 978-1-62944-065-1 (pbk.) | ISBN 978-1-62944-066-8 (eBook) | LCCN 2016902416.
Summary: Two pigs sail around the world. Along the way they befriend a sea serpent and make enemies of the Ice King, a massive polar bear.
Subjects: LCSH Pigs--Juvenile fiction. | Sailing ships--History--19th century--Juvenile fiction. | Fantasy fiction. | Action and adventure stories. | BISAC JUVENILE FICTION / Action & Adventure / General | JUVENILE FICTION / Fantasy & Magic | JUVENILE FICTION / Historical / United States / 19th Century.
Classification: LCC PZ7.P27816 Li 2016 | DCC 813.6--dc23

They that go down to the sea in ships
that do business in great waters;
These see the works of the Lord,
and his wonders in the deep.

—PSALMS 107: 23-24 (KJV)

TABLE OF CONTENTS

1

THE RED WAGON

The grand adventure began quite simply. Just as the rooster crowed, a wagon bounced, bounced, bounced into the farmyard.

The kitchen door slammed and Farmer MacDonald stepped outside to greet the driver. Waving his arms, the farmer guided the wagon backwards, toward the pigsty.

The racket woke the piglets with a start. Predictably, the foolish things squealed. Eeee! Eeee! Eeee!

"Shush," said the sleepy sow. "Shush." She lay on her side and let the piglets root about for breakfast. They soon quieted.

Penelope Grace, the yearling pig, ignored the silly piglets and leaned over the sty to watch the wagon, wide-eyed and curious. Where had the wagon come from? Where did the road lead? What lay beyond her sty and the farm? None of the other farm animals cared about such things. But for Penelope, these questions were like an itch that needed scratching.

It was a red wagon with weathered gray wooden railings around the back, so Penelope couldn't see inside. Last year, her littermates had been herded into a wagon like this, and they disappeared; she didn't know where they went, or, worse, why they left her behind. Her mother's new litter of piglets had been born this spring. She worried: would the piglets be taken away now?

When the wagon was almost touching the sty, the farmer signaled the driver to stop. The farmer took the top pole off the sty. Then he paused, pushed back his straw hat, and scratched his head. "Maybe I'd better section off part of it first."

"Yep. Good idea," the wagon driver said.

The farmer walked around the sty, inspecting it. Finally, he pointed: "The corner might be too dry. No mud. But it'll do for now."

It'll do for what? Curiosity pulled Penelope a step closer.

The wagon's interior was dark, but something was moving, dark against dark. Penelope shivered.

The hound barked, probably roused by the farmer looking for something in the barn. Instinct made Penelope drop back into the sty; even a casual bark from that beast could make her knees quake. Fortunately, the hound was busy with her pups, which left her little time these days to harass pigs.

The farmer came back with three long poles. The sty was already too small for the huge family. In the largest section, the sow, her piglets and Penelope slept. A smaller section held the boar. Now, the farmer inserted the poles into the sides of the sty cutting into the boar's pen by a third to create a small triangular section.

The farmer lowered the wagon's tailgate and positioned a flat board from the tailgate to the inside of the triangle.

"All right, then," the driver said and climbed inside the back of the wagon.

Something white flashed across the dark interior. Trembling, Penelope backed away.

A fresh smell, like the farmyard just after a rain, swept over the sty. Onto the tailgate stepped a black and white pig. A slanting ray of sunshine made his coat gleam. Against the black flashed touches of white: a white-tipped tail, a white forehead-blaze, and four white stocking feet. He hesitated, and then trotted—click, click, click, click—down the ramp into his new home.

With a clatter, the farmer removed the ramp and closed the tailgate. The red wagon bounced away down the road. Farmer MacDonald stretched, yawned, and walked to his house. "Breakfast ready?" he called. The kitchen door slammed and silence fell on the farmyard.

All Penelope could do was stare in fascination. Penelope, herself, was a black and white pig. Like the rest of the Hampshire pigs on the farm, she had a white band wrapped around her body just at her front legs. White front legs sandwiched between black hind legs and black face.

This new pig looked to be a yearling like her, but his markings were all wrong. That white-tipped tail especially, well, it looked wrong. That's all.

Her father rose heavily and shook himself. A head taller than the yearling, the white whiskers on his triple chin quavered with each step. With a confident air, he took his time ambling over to inspect the young boar. He grumbled, "What's this? He's not a Hampshire."

"No, sir. My name is Santiago Talbert." The yearling boar lifted his nose and stood straighter. "And I'm a Berkshire."

The old boar shook himself, deliberately splattering mud onto Santiago's gleaming coat. "Don't know what Farmer MacDonald wants with you."

"I don't know either, sir." Santiago rubbed his front leg against the pole, trying to wipe off the mud. "But don't worry. I'm not staying that long. I plan to sail the Seven Seas."

"Sail?" guffawed the old boar. "Pigs don't sail."

Santiago lifted his chin in defiance. "This pig will."

Penelope caught her breath. She had grown up listening to Mrs. MacDonald recite poetry. Mrs. MacDonald read aloud from new poetry books while milking Consuela, the nanny goat. She recited poetry while gathering the biddy-hens' eggs. She memorized lines of poetry—by repeating them endlessly—while mucking out the barn and sty. Penelope's favorite poems were about the high seas. But pigs don't sail.

Or do they?

Penelope's world suddenly expanded. "Sail? Will you take me with you?"

Santiago turned and met Penelope's gaze, the first time their eyes actually met. And Love-at-First-Sight struck them both.

2

CHOICES

Santiago pressed against the poles separating him from Penelope. "What's your name?"

"Penelope Grace."

"Ah. It suits you. Penelope Grace."

When he said her name, it sounded smooth, and she liked that. "What kind of pig are you?"

"We're a royal breed." He spoke with obvious pride. "Queen Victoria, herself–Queen of England–bred the first Berkshire. She named him Ace of Spades. Since then, we've spread around the world. I'm surprised I'm the first you've seen."

"Stuck up, pig," murmured the sow. Mud squelched faintly as she rolled over. In the summer heat, she loved a good mud bath to stay cool. "Penelope, get away from him."

Obediently, Penelope moved far away from Santiago's small pen to the opposite side of the sty. But the sow's comment stirred up the boar, too. Though he was past his prime and his muscles were melting into fat, he was still strong. He charged at the poles that separated him from Santiago.

Bam! The fence held.

The old boar paced stiff-legged, his head high, in a show of aggression meant to show that he was boss. But the cool mud called, and soon he returned to his mud hole to sleep after all the morning's excitement. His grunty snores filled the farmyard.

Santiago didn't strike Penelope as a foolhardy pig; he stayed as far away from the old boar as possible. But Santiago didn't stand down completely, either. He held his head up and repeated the Berkshire story to every farm animal and sparrow that asked.

Obediently, Penelope stayed away from Santiago that morning, though her eyes never left him. She could be patient and wait for her mother to sleep. Then she would talk to Santiago.

At noon, the farmer's grandchildren trooped out of the house lugging buckets of slops. The smell reached the sty first, and the boar stumbled to his food trough half-asleep. Squealing, the piglets tried to reach the trough in their pen. The jumbled smells caught Penelope, and she pushed aside piglets so she could eat. She took a bite, closed her eyes, and chewed.

From behind her, though, came a high-pitched squealing that wouldn't stop. Eee! Eee! Eee! Almost without thinking, she shoved sideways, pushing the piglets down the trough. Runt squeezed into the space she had created.

Meanwhile, the children had put down a separate bucket for Santiago. They stayed to poke and prod him.

"He's pretty. For a pig," said the tallest child.

At this, they all giggled.

Santiago whirled to snap at a stick that poked his back.

Luckily for Santiago, Mrs. McDonald rang the lunch bell, and the grandchildren scrambled back to the house.

All the attention toward the new pig stirred up the boar again. Once or twice every hour, he paced along the poles that kept him from the yearling, stopping often to slam—bam!—into the poles. The fence held throughout the afternoon.

That evening, when the sow and the boar and the piglets were finally snoring, Penelope Grace crept to the edge of Santiago's pen. She had tried to hold her expectations in check, but she was brimming with questions. She called softly, "Are you awake?"

"Yes."

While stars spun around the North Star, they talked, and as they talked, Penelope realized just how lonely she'd been this past year on the farm with no one who shared her crazy dreams. Yes, they talked. About the Seven Seas. About what was beyond the farm and the woods and where the road led. Santiago told her he was raised on a farm about an hour's ride away by the wagon. At that farm, there were lots of breeds of pigs: Hampshires, Berkshires, Durocs, Poland Chinas, and Whites. He didn't know much about the countryside between farms because he hadn't seen out of the red wagon.

"But the robins and crows and songbirds have told me," Santiago said, "that beyond this countryside you can cross a river into a different world. It's a place where an intelligent creature—animal or human—can get ahead."

"What does that mean?"

"I don't know, exactly. But I can't stay here. What kind of future do I have?"

"What does that mean?"

"Eventually, we all become bacon."

The statement stunned Penelope. Of course. Pigs on a farm meant bacon. And when the wagon took away her brothers and sisters last year, they went. . . Penelope sank to her knees. Her brothers and sisters were bacon.

Why hadn't her mother explained? Of course. To keep her from fretting about things she couldn't change.

But Santiago had more to say: "I know why Farmer MacDonald bought me, even if your father doesn't."

"How could you know?"

"When they loaded me into the red wagon this morning, I heard my farmer and the wagon driver talking. Look at how old the boar and the sow are."

"So?"

"They are almost done having babies. I'm supposed to replace him and sire lots of piglets."

"With my mother?" Penelope was outraged.

Santiago just looked at her.

"Oh." And Penelope understood then why she was left behind when her siblings were taken away. She was supposed to replace her mother and raise piglets to be sent to become bacon. The horror of it took her breath away. She loved her mother, but babies had sapped away her mother's life. Penelope wanted babies, of course, but not a new litter each year to become bacon.

"I'll wind up like him." Santiago nodded toward the old boar. "Living for my mud. That's no life."

"We don't have a choice. It's what pigs do. Isn't it?"

"Not this pig." Santiago tilted his head up toward the spangled sky.

Penelope followed his gaze. A gentle wind swept through the farmyard, bringing a strange new smell. Was it a new flower? Or a new grass? Or a creature she'd never seen before? Oh, to go new places and see new things. Maybe it was possible. It was a new thought, a new emotion, and it grew quickly. She thought: *this is what it feels like to have hope.*

She tested this new emotion, this hope. Was she going to stay here and let the farmer breed her every year, then send her babies off to become bacon?

No. There had to be other choices.

Santiago's voice was strong. "I don't know what the wider world is like, but I'm going to find out. And I know how to get there! Let me draw you a map."

"What's a map?"

Santiago's eyes shone in the starlight. "The birds told me about maps. I love maps. They are drawings that show the world. Look." With his right front hoof, he smoothed the dirt and then drew squares. "This is our countryside, and this squiggly line is the river we have to cross to reach the wider world. Farther on there are a few states or countries, or whatever they are called. And then, the ocean. It'll be easy to find the ocean."

Penelope's eyes grew wide with admiration. "It's a beautiful map. Lines and squares and the ocean. You know so much about the world."

"Not enough," Santiago said. He studied his crude map and shook his head.

Maybe he didn't know enough, Penelope thought. To make it in the wider world, they would need to take risks. They might fail once, twice, or even thrice. They might be in danger. They might go hungry. They might have difficulties Penelope couldn't even begin to imagine. Fear of these risks made her tremble deep in her pig bones; she wanted to be safe. Yet she feared failure more. If she decided not to take the risks, she had already failed.

"Do you know enough to get us to the ocean? So we can find a sail boat?"

Santiago shrugged. "Yes."

"Then you know enough." Of all the things she had ever said, Penelope thought this was the bravest.

3

ESCAPE

Now, it's all very well to know about the wider world. Escaping from a pigsty is another matter. Penelope and Santiago talked about escape every night, but they had no idea how to get out of the sty. They couldn't climb over because pigs can't climb; they couldn't dig under because pigs can't dig.

"Be patient," Penelope advised. "We'll figure it out."

The only bright spot in their days was the farmer's wife reciting poetry while she worked. She was memorizing Coleridge's "Rime of the Ancient Mariner," a story of tragedy on the high seas. The stirring words hardened Santiago's and Penelope's resolve. "We will sail."

Yet Penelope was also having second thoughts. What would the wider world be like? All she knew was this farm. Sometimes when Santiago talked about leaving, a shiver of fear ran down her spine. The outside world was a vast unknown. If they could leave tonight, would she go? It's one thing to know you have choices; it's another thing to make the right choices.

Meanwhile, lunchtime became a torture. The grandchildren loved to play cruel tricks on the pigs, especially the oldest grandchild. Skinny Yates liked to climb on the sty's fence posts, then balance and walk the cross-pole to the next post. The other grandchildren shouted their approval. For each successful trip from post to post, Yates rewarded himself by stopping and throwing things at the old boar. Small sticks, old corn cobs, clumps of dirt, or acorns.

He just wallowed deeper in the mud and ignored Yates, so Yates switched to throwing things at the piglets. They squealed and ran about, making the grandchildren squeal and run about, too.

But one day the farmer caught Yates throwing a corncob at a scared piglet. He whipped his grandson and told him to leave the piglets alone. But the farmer didn't say anything about yearlings.

Penelope at least had a larger pen to run around in. Or she could lie amongst the piglets, and Yates couldn't try for her. Santiago, however, had no mud in which to wallow and no place to hide in his tiny corner sty. While Yates played, Santiago stayed alert, dodging the inevitable missiles. And Yates grew madder and madder as his throws missed.

One day, the grandchildren laughed and teased Yates. "What's wrong? Can't you hit him?"

Yates disappeared into the woods and came back with a stack of bigger sticks to set beside Santiago's sty. He picked up one in each hand and climbed the fence post.

Santiago backed as far away as possible, but he couldn't escape.

Yates threw.

"You got him!" one grandchild yelled.

Santiago charged at Yates, slamming into the sty poles. Yates had nothing to worry about; the sty was sturdy and would hold against even the old boar's charges. Santiago lapsed into a sullen anger. He turned his back to the children and buried his head in the corner of his sty.

The grandchildren laughed, and Yates threw more sticks. At least ten sticks were direct hits on Santiago's back.

Penelope hated Yates's smile of triumph. She didn't know how Santiago took it all so calmly. He just sat and took it until the sticks were all spent. Because he refused to react, eventually the children became bored and left.

That night, Santiago refused to sleep. "Not till I find a way out of this sty," he muttered to Penelope.

He worked on the fence, shoving poles up, then down, banging them around in his frustration.

Penelope studied the poles, trying to figure out how they worked. Tilting her head, she suggested, "Try pushing that pole toward my father."

Surprised by her suggestion, Santiago said, "You understand things, don't you? Together, we will figure this out."

Pleased with the comment, Penelope urged him on. "Try it."

Santiago braced his hind legs and shoved the cross-pole in the direction Penelope had indicated. "It moved!" he cried. He pushed and pushed until the pole almost fell out of the fence posts. "Look! If I can do that to the top two poles, I'll be able to escape."

Astonished, Penelope whispered, "We're going to sea."

But the old sow pushed Penelope down and studied the fence poles herself. "I've been watching you. I know what you're planning to do. You think you want adventure?" she said to Santiago.

Penelope worried; she wanted her mother's approval, but she was determined to leave, no matter what.

"Of course, we want adventure," Santiago said.

"It'll make you happy?"

"Yes." The white blaze on Santiago's forehead wrinkled in confusion.

"And you want to take Penelope with you?"

"Yes, ma'am," Santiago stood straighter. "Together, we'll have a life of adventure."

"Come here," the sow commanded. "I don't see very well."

Santiago walked closer, but the sow waved her foreleg for him to come even closer. He finally stopped a nose-length away.

Penelope held her breath. The night sounds were familiar: her father's snores, the barn owl's hoots, and the crickets' chirps. Would she get to leave it all behind?

The sow squinted. Her dark eyes wrinkled with the effort, leaving dark furrowed shadows, like a mask of suspicion. "You're so confident," she scorned.

"No. So desperate," Santiago murmured so low that Penelope barely heard.

"Ah." The sow's face cleared. "That's why you'll succeed."

Penelope felt like dancing across the cross-pole herself; her mother approved of Santiago. Penelope put her front hooves back on the top pole, so she was shoulder to shoulder with the sow. Together, they studied the Berkshire pig. Did her mother see what she saw? To Penelope, Santiago wasn't just another pig. She liked his new ideas, his sense of adventure, and his willingness to go new places. And she understood his desperation because she felt it, too. "We'll be okay, Mother. The wider world will be—well, more than life in a sty."

"Much more," Santiago said with confidence.

The sow nodded. "Excitement alone might be enough at first. But in the end, you know, you'll want more. When the excitement wears off, remember this: how you live your life is more important than having adventures." At their skeptical looks, she broke off. "Ah, but you won't listen to me." She dropped down from the fence, waddled back to her piglets, and lay down again.

Penelope whispered to Santiago. "Let's go. Right now."

"No. I want one more showdown with Yates."

"Why?"

"When I escape, they'll look for me—for us. If we can make it look like Yates' fault, they won't look so hard for us. Instead, they'll just fuss at him."

Against his black hide, Penelope couldn't see the bruises from Yates stick throwing, but she knew there were many. It was only fair that Yates took the blame. "Escape. That's the important thing."

"Yes," Santiago agreed. "I'll be free."

"We'll be free," Penelope echoed.

Penelope couldn't shove the sty poles from her section because they were longer and heavier. She had no choice but to wait for Santiago to choose the time. But she worried about Santiago's desire for revenge.

The next day, the sun was so brilliant and hot that even Penelope was forced to squirm into the muck to keep cool. Santiago had only the thin shade of the fence, so he paced around his triangle first from east to west, then west to east. As the heat grew, the biddy-hens settled in dusty spots, and the lambs dozed in fitful morning naps. Only the angry drone of bees filled the farmyard. It was like the entire farm was watching, waiting. Mud caked and cracked on Penelope's back, and still Santiago paced, hot and miserable and determined. Finally, when the sun was directly overhead, Penelope heard the kitchen door slam.

Santiago positioned himself by the sty post, his front legs fixed and stiff. The grandchildren lugged four buckets of slops to the sty. Yates wasn't carrying a bucket. Instead, he pranced ahead and leaned on the fence to study Santiago.

"Today, pig," he said, "I'll get you good." He patted his pockets, which were bulging.

Dark eyes glittering, Santiago gazed steadily at the boy.

The other grandchildren poured lunch into the troughs and watched the piglets erupt from the mud. Then they waited for the real show to start.

Watching Yates pull a pine cone from his pocket, Penelope felt a sudden tenderness. For all their talk, she and Santiago might never have made the effort to escape without Yates. They had needed his goading to get past their fears of the outside world. In an odd way, he'd done them a favor by mistreating Santiago. And now, the—what did Mrs. MacDonald call him?—the "dear boy" would get what he deserved.

Yates wiped his hands on his overalls and climbed up the sty post. His bare feet were dusty, but his skinny toes clung to the narrow cross-pole. He held his hands out for balance and danced lightly to the middle of the pole. Then he hefted two pinecones.

Santiago rose on his hind legs and put his hooves on the cross-pole.

Yates drew back an arm and took aim.

Santiago shoved the pole. It fell, toppling Yates.

"Get out!" Penelope yelled. "Go!"

Santiago shoved the second pole and it fell, too, right on top of Yates. The young boar dodged Yates, who was struggling to sit up, and then stepped over the bottom pole. Santiago turned back to Penelope. "Look for me by moonlight."

"By moonlight," Penelope promised.

By the time Yates managed to stand, Santiago was off and running. He led Yates and the grandchildren on a merry chase. Through the chicken yard—Squawk!—where white feathers flew. Under the sheep fence—Baa!—scattering the lambs around their pasture and back out again. Finally, Santiago dashed for the woods and disappeared.

Penelope was left to worry. She hung over the sty fence, trying to see what was happening, until her legs ached and her chest was sore from rubbing the pole. Where was Santiago?

About mid-afternoon, Yates and the grandchildren trudged back, empty handed, to the farmhouse. The kitchen door slammed—Bam, Bam, Bam, Bam, Bam—as each child took their turn going inside.

The wind stirred the trees and bushes at the edge of the woods. Where was Santiago? Was he safe? Penelope's gaze darted from bush to bush.

At last she saw his head poke out of a bush, nod once, and then disappear. Penelope sighed with satisfaction. When the moon rose that night, she would be free. Suddenly, Penelope realized she'd been so worried she hadn't eaten lunch. She dropped down and trotted over to snuffle at the scraps the piglets had left.

A few minutes later, Farmer MacDonald stomped out to stand and glare at the empty triangle of the pigsty. "You'll have to find him."

Head hanging, Yates stood barefoot beside him. "He's long gone by now."

"Maybe the old sow and boar still have a couple more litters in them," the Farmer said. "They've never caused me any trouble."

Penelope caught her breath. Maybe their escape would gain her parents a longer life.

Yates said nothing.

"Berkshires are the Queen's breed, you know. Expensive," the farmer said. "Find him. Or, you'll pay." The farmer slapped the boy's back.

Yates could do nothing but nod. When Farmer MacDonald went back in the house, Yates went back into the woods. For several hours, she heard him yelling and stomping about, but Santiago was well hidden.

When Mrs. MacDonald called Yates for supper, he went inside and stayed.

Night came softly. Penelope watched for Santiago, and he came for her by moonlight. But Penelope hung back, worried.

"Did you see Yates crying behind the hen house?" she asked.

Santiago hung his head. "Yes. I'm sad for him, but it was the best way to get free. You heard the farmer. He'll make Yates pay, and that means they'll stop looking for us."

Was that right or wrong? Penelope didn't know enough about the world to decide. For now, she was just ready to leave this old sty behind.

Together, they shoved the top cross-pole out of her section of the sty. It fell with a clatter. A thrill of fear shot through Penelope. It would wake the farmer! Or the dog! Or her father!

But her father's grunty snores held steady. The farmhouse and farmyard were still.

An owl called from the woods. Penelope flinched, but said steadily, "Try the next pole."

Santiago shoved at the second pole, but somehow it caught.

"Climb over," Santiago urged.

"Pigs don't climb."

"Sailors climb up and down ropes. If we're going to sail, we've got to learn."

So Penelope gritted her teeth and put her front hooves on the second pole. She heaved, but fell back. Oddly, she felt something under her rump, pushing. She scrambled until her back legs found the bottom pole. Then she shoved hard. She fell over the sty poles, onto her snout. Her eyes teared up in pain, but she shook it off. She was out of the pigsty for the first time in her life! Free!

Turning, she saw Runt looking through the bottom poles. Maybe all the piglets weren't as silly as they sounded.

"Thanks." Impulsively, she whispered to Runt, "There's a wider world, and we're going to find it. Make sure you escape before the red wagon comes back in the fall. Ask the birds. They know where to find the wider world." It was hard leaving her family behind knowing their fate, but warning him was all she could do.

"I'll find the wider world," Runt said confidently. "If you can do it, so can I." With that, he scampered back to the pack of piglets.

"You'll have to learn to climb better than that," Santiago said. "We can practice while we cross the countryside and find the ocean. Come."

"Wait." Penelope turned back to the sty one last time.

The old sow rose, shaking off the piglets. Like a boat in heavy seas, she listed from side to side as she waddled to the edge of the sty. "You're leaving me, then, dearie?"

Santiago hung back and let them talk.

"Oh, mother, it's the life I've dreamed of: poetry, music, maps, adventure."

"Do it right," her mother said fiercely. "For all of us."

Penelope understood; she would be the only one to escape the common fate of all pigs on farms, the only one to have a bright future.

"It makes my heart full to hear you talk of ture." Her mother's voice broke, and tears filled her eyes. "Full with the joy we've had in this pigsty, and empty with the joy at letting you go make your way in the wider world."

No, Penelope thought. *I won't be the only one to live a full life*. Amazingly, her mother had done that, even here on the farm. Penelope studied her with a new respect.

The old sow continued: "When you finally settle down and have piglets of your own, will you name one after me?"

The plump old sow was wrinkled and tired-looking, as usual. But she had always stood by Penelope, making sure she had milk and slops, even though she had to fight eight other brothers and sisters. "I don't think I know your name. You're just— Mother."

"Victoria Marie."

In the starlight, her mother's damp eyelashes looked long and thick, her eyes soft and deep. Victoria Marie must have been a beautiful piglet and yearling.

The sow turned back to her sleeping piglets.

Penelope called, her voice rough with emotion, "I love you, Victoria Marie."

"I love you, Penelope Grace." The sow gave Penelope a gentle smile, then nosed the piglets and lay down beside them with a sigh.

Santiago turned his face, again, toward the eastern star, and Penelope followed as he led the way toward the deep blue sea.

4

HUNGRY

Santiago Talbert and Penelope Grace were married by the first owl they met in a brief but satisfying ceremony, with ten bats and two raccoons as witnesses. Afterward, they danced with joy under the North Star till dawn, and then slept for the day.

For the next month, the Talberts traveled east toward the river and the wider world, traveling by night and sleeping by day. Anticipation filled Penelope each evening. Perhaps tonight they would crest a rise, and before them would lie the great river. And tomorrow, maybe they would be in the wider world. As the days passed, the anticipation grew; surely the previous night's journey had taken them even closer to their goal. Tonight, yes, tonight, they would find the river.

Meanwhile, they reveled in the new world they were exploring. The open road smelled different: no pigsty, no food trough with old bits of slops, no dogs, no chickens, no horses, no people. Instead, there was the smell of green: grass, bushes, trees. It was a heady smell that both excited and scared them.

But green wasn't the only smell that intrigued them; they investigated each new smell. That's how they found their first acorns, a sweet delicacy they came to crave. That's how they first met—and ran away from—a skunk family. That's how they found spicy marigolds near a farmhouse.

It was nearing midnight, before moonrise, and the black sky crawled with pinpricks of light. Penelope followed her nose to a new scent and found a bed of yellow-gold flowers. The first bite was sharp, yet sweet.

"Santiago, over here!"

Santiago's dark and white form trotted around the corner of the house. Penelope eagerly turned. But wait, it wasn't Santiago—the smell was wrong. Penelope squinted. She chewed the flower again, and then stopped. It wasn't Santiago. A trembling started deep inside, and she spat out the flower. She took a deep breath.

That thing smelled of—dog.

The beagle bayed, his voice deep and demanding, an alarm for the family who was sleeping inside.

With her stomach heaving in fear, Penelope spun and trotted away. The beagle's voice took up a different cry. She glanced around; he was gaining on her. Putting on a burst of speed, dust kicked up and stuck in her throat. She struggled to breath. Dogs had strong yellow teeth that sank into muscle, and they never let go. Faster, she needed to go faster. Her hooves bit into the soft dirt. Was he still behind her? She gasped for breath.

Suddenly, white light glared over the farmyard. A door slammed. The beagle ran to its master. In the bright light, Penelope saw he was tied to a long rope.

Her breathing eased, and she slowed, but fear kept her moving.

Santiago trotted up beside her. "I wish he'd been loose. Hide-and-seek with Yates that last day was fun. Berkshires love that sort of thing."

Which frustrated Penelope even more. Santiago liked hide-and-seek? Even watching it made her jittery. If that dog had chased her, he'd easily catch her. How could Santiago laugh about that kind of danger?

A sudden cramp in her hind leg made Penelope pull up. Still, she limped on, fear pushing her hard, until they could no longer see the lights of the farm.

"Will dogs always be tied up?" Penelope's voice trembled. She shook her hind leg trying to ease the lingering cramp.

"At night, probably," Santiago said. "It really bothers you?"

"Yes." It was all she could manage to say.

"Should we avoid farms from now on?" Santiago sounded disappointed.

Penelope tested her leg by standing heavily on it. The cramp was almost gone. From the corner of her eye, she studied Santiago. This whole journey was a dangerous, high stakes gamble. Did she really want to go to sea with a Berkshire who liked to provoke dogs?

Dogs. One night long ago, when Penelope was just a piglet, a fox broke into the hen house. She remembered how the biddy-hens set up a squawking and clucking. The rooster started to crow in indignation, but it was cut short. Cock-a-

Dwauk! Silence. The fox had killed the rooster. Then the ruckus started again as the fox chased the widowed hens.

The farmyard hound arrived, baying. The farmer flung open the henhouse door, and the hound bounded inside. Smart hens flew to the rafters, away from the fight. After the hound had caught and killed the fox, it started sniffing around. It followed the fox's trail into the woods. Not far into the woods—still in sight of the pigsty so that Penelope had a good view—he started digging. He dug rapidly and soon dragged out tiny fox kits. Three of them.

Then the hound played.

One kit tried to escape, but the hound slapped it with his huge paw, knocking it over. The kit rolled back toward the exposed den; to prevent it escaping back underground, the hound snapped its neck.

Penelope had squealed in anger. But hers had been just one of the many noises on the farm that night. Mrs. MacDonald was crying over the dead rooster. The horses were kicking their stalls. The grandchildren were screaming about how foxes were wild. Over all of it, the hens were crying in grief. CLUCK, Cluck, cluck, cluck. CLUCK, Cluck, cluck, cluck.

The next kit the hound slapped around a bit longer, keeping it on level ground. After one tremendous slap, the kit didn't get up again. The hound put a paw on the kit and tore at its fur. The third kit was whimpering pitifully, walking in circles. The hound knocked it around as well, letting it race a few steps before slapping it down.

Penelope screamed, "Let it go."

But it, too, fell and didn't get up. When the hound looked up, his jaws were full of fur.

Dogs. Cruel hounds. The memory of that night still haunted Penelope.

"Yes," she said firmly to Santiago. "We should avoid farms and dogs."

The decision meant slower progress, but it eased Penelope's fears of the open road.

Over the next week, they passed through gently rolling cornfields, which seemed to stretch for miles and miles. When would they reach the river? Perhaps it was just beyond the cornfields. The ears of corn were still small and tight, waiting for the cool of autumn to ripen. From an eagle's eye view, the land was just large squares of crops. Only slight variations in color kept each square distinct from the last. For two pigs who knew nothing about foraging, there was nothing in the farmlands to eat.

They traveled at a steady pace, continually moving east, while the moon tracked across the sky. Penelope's stomach rumbled louder and louder. When the moon finally set, Penelope halted. "I'm hungry."

"Berkshires are tough." Santiago stripped long leaves from a corn plant and chewed with determination.

Penelope glared. She was still surprised sometimes at how different a Berkshire looked from Hampshire pigs like her. She thought the white band around the front legs of Hampshires was clean looking. Santiago just had white stocking feet, a white blaze on his forehead and a white-tipped tail.

And he looked ludicrous chewing a corn plant, like a cow chewing its cud.

"Of course Hampshires are tough, too," Santiago said quickly.

Penelope stalked stiff-legged down a row of corn. *Stuck-up pig*, she thought.

"But Berkshires can put up with things. Like hunger." Santiago ambled after her.

Penelope whirled around and pressed her black snout against Santiago's white snout. She said tightly, "I'm sick of Berkshires."

Santiago held his ground. "Don't insult me."

"Berkshire this. Berkshire that."

Santiago drew himself up. "Berkshires always say–"

"Not again."

In the silence, an owl screeched. He was probably gulping down a baby mouse or some other tasty tidbit. Penelope thought with longing of the aroma of warm slops; back home, good food had appeared when she was hungry. She hadn't realized how much the comforts of home meant to her. Leaving home–leaving everything familiar–was just plain hard. Nothing was comfortable.

Traveling, it was so hard to remember that she liked Santiago, and she should be nice to him even when she didn't want to. Wait–maybe she'd gone too far. "It's all I hear," she said, but softer this time. She turned and trotted along the cornrow again.

Santiago followed, but they were both silent for a few minutes.

Penelope's stomach growled. "I'm hungry."

"So find something." His voice was kinder.

"Where? Corn plants are so tasteless. So boring."

So low she almost didn't hear, Santiago asked, "Are Berkshires boring, too?"

Penelope sighed. "No. Just so proud."

"I'm not what you bargained for."

Penelope stopped to face him. With a fierceness that surprised her, she said, "No. You're better than I bargained for."

Santiago swaggered, then, showing off. "And Berkshires are special?"

The stars—except the morning star—were all fading. It was near dawn. "I'm not what you bargained for either?" she asked.

Santiago rubbed alongside her. "Hampshires are special, too."

Suddenly, it didn't matter that they were both hungry. They were together and heading for the wider world, and life was good. And maybe tomorrow night, they'd find the great river.

They spent a hungry day sleeping along a fencerow where vines and shrubs created some cover. About midnight the next night, they came to a creek where large oaks and cottonwood trees spread their branches. They foraged on early acorns until the ache in their bellies eased.

A sudden commotion caught their attention. A shadow darted past. Penelope swiveled her head to follow a tiny bird. It swooped around in another wide, shallow, U-shaped flight, then dove. Penelope studied the shrub where the bird had disappeared.

The bird burst out of the shrub, built up speed in another circling flight, and dove.

Santiago crouched and looked under the shrub, then straightened. "A snake is attacking the hummingbird's nest. Looks like a speckled king snake."

Penelope crouched, too, and studied the nest. It was tiny, not even half as wide as her front hoof. Soft, camouflage-colored materials were stuck together with spider webbing and molded into a cup shape. Two fledglings, almost the size of their mother, jumped about, their sharp bills jutting here and there, as if they would stab any intruder. Blinking, Penelope thought, all hummingbird babies are runts.

The king snake had already climbed about halfway up the shrub. His dark eyes were fixed on the babies, his supper.

"Do something," Penelope snapped.

Santiago shrugged. "There's nothing we can do. It's a snake."

"Those baby birds want to live. My mother said–and Berkshires should agree–how we live is more important than having adventures. We didn't come here just to live like pigs in a sty. We can do something."

"What?"

In another flash of red and green, the hummingbird mother dove desperately at the king snake.

Obviously, Santiago had no idea what to do. Penelope gritted her teeth in anger. She didn't know either, but she had to try something. She crouched and crept forward, trying to mimic the barnyard cat; her ears were flat, and her eyes intent. Like lightning, she leapt, bit the snake's tail and jerked; its hold on the shrub loosened, and Penelope stumbled backward.

Oh! She had a fat snake in her mouth!

Santiago's eyes were wide with surprise.

With a snap of her head, Penelope slammed the speckled snake into the water. Splash! It glided jerkily—as if trying to recover from being thrown about—to the creek's other side and into the undergrowth.

Santiago whistled slowly. "Wow!"

Penelope drew a shaky breath and grinned. It was a good thing she hadn't thought about it before attacking the snake.

Santiago spat at the snake's disappearing tail. "It'll come back, though."

The hummingbird, her red breast flashing, hovered in front of Penelope's face. She dipped and wove about in a dance of thanks. Penelope pushed aside leaves and peered at the red just showing on the fledglings' breasts. "They look like they're almost big enough to leave the nest." She turned back to the mother. "Teach them to fly today. Or that king snake will have his supper after all."

The hummingbird dipped and disappeared into the shrub.

Penelope sighed. "Think they'll make it?"

"At least you gave them a chance," Santiago said.

The land changed as they traveled on, growing flatter. Surely the great river was just ahead. The anticipation that had carried Penelope thus far gave way to a nagging worry:

what if this was all for nothing, and there was no wider world? Or what if they couldn't get to this mysterious place? How would they cross the river? Was just anyone allowed to cross?

They grew even leaner and stringier the next few weeks as they avoided all farmyards, chicken houses, barns and stables. Foraging was decent, but they always carried an edge of hunger. Hunger not just for food, but also for a sight of the great river. Now, Penelope hurried up each rise, stopping to scan ahead. They had come so far; the river had to be near.

One night, they came to a creek and the local watering hole, a deep, clear pool. They decided to spend the night asking if anyone knew the way to the wider world.

Nearby, a bullfrog chug-a-rumped. Branches rattled in the wind. And the wind had picked up.

A raccoon jumped from a tree and climbed onto a rotten log. His agile hands picked up acorns and chunked them into the dark hole in the log. Like an old man fussing, a porcupine rattled out of the log, scolding the raccoon for disturbing him. The raccoon chattered back, then leapt over the porcupine's quills and scampered to Penelope and Santiago.

"You're new."

Santiago said, "We've come a long ways."

The raccoon dashed to the creek, washed an acorn, and galumphed back to them. "You're passing through?" He was as large as a sheepdog and spoke with a strange accent.

"We're looking for the wider world."

The raccoon sat back on his haunches. His strong jaws cracked the acorn, and he crunched delicately on it. "Now there's something you don't hear often. Why would you want to go there?"

Santiago told their story of escape from the farm and of their adventures on the way. The raccoon was most interested in the story about scaring the snake away from the hummingbird nest.

"Why did you help her?"

Penelope said, "How you treat others is more important than having adventures." She couldn't help looking over at the log where the porcupine was still scratching about and muttering to himself. Teasing the porcupine had been rude of the raccoon, but she was too polite to say that.

The raccoon asked lots of questions, but he didn't tell much about himself. "You don't sound like you're from here," Penelope said.

"You're right. I've been to the wider world."

Lightning cracked overhead.

"What's it like there?" Penelope asked eagerly.

Santiago pushed forward, "How do you get there?"

The raccoon tossed aside the acorn shell. "Rain's coming soon. You don't have much time. Listen. This stream runs into the Mississippi River in another mile. If you just try to swim across, you'll still be in this world." He shook his head. "Some try that when they aren't allowed across."

Penelope's heart felt tight. Some animals weren't allowed to cross. She didn't have time to ask "why not?" The raccoon was already turning away.

As he scampered away, the raccoon called back, "To cross, you must take the ferry. It's just south of here. To reach the wider world, you must cross on that ferry."

Then, before Penelope could say anything, the raccoon clambered up a cottonwood where the pigs glimpsed two other raccoons waiting for him.

"Come back!" Santiago cried.

The raccoon called, "Once you cross into the wider world, you can't come back. Think hard before you cross." Then it disappeared into branches that were flapping about in the wind.

Turning to Penelope, Santiago cried, "We're close!"

"Almost there." Penelope's eyes tingled with tears. But the raccoon's words had scared her; some creatures weren't allowed to cross. What did that mean? How did they stop creatures from crossing? Who stopped them?

"Once we cross, we can't come back," Santiago repeated.

Penelope realized the raccoon told them how to cross to the wider world, but he didn't tell them anything about the wider world itself. Hope had carried her for so long, but it was hope in a dream that was hard to touch. What was the wider world like? Did she and Santiago really want to go there? Would they be allowed to go? They could stay here and just live wild. It would be a good life, wouldn't it?

But Santiago had ambitions of getting ahead in the world. He often said, "It's not money or fame or power that I want. I want a challenge to conquer. I want to make a difference in the lives of a few creatures."

For Penelope, it was simpler than that. She wanted to go to the wider world because the unknown called her. And in spite of her fears or her worries about the crossing, she had to answer that call, she had to know what lay beyond this river. "Can't come back? Or won't want to?"

Santiago shrugged. "It amounts to the same thing."

5

IN NEED OF COINS

Amidst growing wind, Penelope and Santiago trotted side by side until they came up a rise, and there, lying before them, was the Mississippi River. Flowing past was the largest stretch of water they'd ever seen. They stood quivering, trying to understand the swift brown water. Penelope edged down the bank until her hooves sank into soft mud. She bent and drank deeply. The thick water rolled around her mouth. The placid surface was a lie; she tasted hints of what must lie beneath the calm. Deep currents stirred and mingled the soil from thousands of farms and forests. She closed her eyes and swallowed the river water. She could almost understand the river's quiet murmurs. The moment passed, and she wished instead for a translator. The mighty river was hundreds of pig troughs across and cradled memories of too many lives for a simple pig to understand.

"If only we had a sail boat," Penelope said.

Santiago shook his head. "I want to explore the seas, not a river."

Strong winds left them no time to linger; they needed to ford before the rains hit. They trotted south and soon saw a wooden dock with a flat-bottomed ferry tied up. Excited, they clattered onto the dock. The wind whipped up waves that slapped against the ferry. The boat was old, its wood stained dark from water and wear. A tiny cabin at the center was lit by a lantern; the cabin was empty. There was room for them.

A red-haired ferryman sat near the tiller with his back toward them.

"I'll ask him about crossing," Santiago whispered.

"He won't understand you."

Santiago cleared his throat. "Sir."

The ferryman didn't answer, but he did understand them. He pointed to a painted sign, which was nailed to a one of the dock posts, just above a lantern, so it was easily seen. It showed a skunk giving a coin to a red-haired man.

Penelope felt a jolt of surprise and excitement. If this man understood them, then the wider world was close, and it was going to be a strange world, indeed. She gulped and spoke directly to the man. "We don't have any coins. We're just animals."

For an answer, the ferryman turned away and flipped his collar up against the rain that started to patter down. Reaching into his jacket pocket, he pulled out a floppy hat and covered his head.

"Will you take us across?" Penelope asked.

Without looking around, the ferryman shook his head.

Penelope was crushed. What she did not want was slop thrown into a trough. What she did not want was a pigsty so tiny she could cross it in five steps. What she did not want were children throwing pinecones at her. What she did not want was a wasted life. They had traveled a lifetime to get here. And now—they weren't going to be allowed to board the ferry? All because they didn't have a coin.

Farmer MacDonald had coins, and once he accidentally dropped a shiny silver coin into the sty. The piglets had stomped it into the mud before Penelope could grab it. She needed that coin now!

Santiago was practical. "We'll find shelter from the rain and figure this out later. We aren't beaten, yet." He nudged Penelope toward the beach.

But Penelope glared at the ferryman. "Uncivilized. Unjust. Unfair."

But the rain washed down her face, and the ferryman said nothing.

Penelope stepped forward and puffed out her chest. "We've as much right to go to the wider world as the next creature. What's to stop us from boarding your ferry anyway?"

The ferryman shrugged. "Go ahead. But you won't get to the wider world unless I steer the boat. That's how it works."

No amount of bravado could solve this problem. Frustrated, the pigs trotted down the echoing boardwalk to the shore. Penelope stopped short. Before them stood a small brown bear and a possum.

"Wouldn't let you on the ferry?" The bear shook her head sadly. She looked past her prime, with white hairs sprinkled on her neck and her muzzle.

Santiago stood between Penelope and the other animals. "No," he said shortly. "We have no coins."

The possum lashed his tail about like an angry whip. "We've been here for a month, trying to figure out how to cross to the wider world."

A month! Penelope swallowed hard. They were so close; they couldn't fail now. "Has anyone crossed this month?"

"No one," growled the bear.

Despair swept through Penelope. Sweet anticipation had marked the early days of their travel. Would it all end here, with disappointment?

She cocked her ears: over the wind's moaning she heard something.

"Dogs," the bear said. "They patrol this part of the river." The bear turned and started to trot away.

The possum said, "They're probably after those raccoons again. The dogs are fast. You better get out of here."

The possum joined the bear, and they disappeared along the banks, in the direction of the watering hole.

Penelope and Santiago hesitated, uncertain of where they could find shelter. Within the few seconds they hesitated, the barking grew louder. It sounded like a wild hunting pack was coming straight for them.

"Let's go." Santiago turned to follow the possum, and Penelope followed Santiago.

Suddenly, out of the shrubs, spurted three raccoons. At their tails, a tall shepherd dog leapt and caught the slowest. Two more shepherds rushed from the shrubs to join him.

It was too late to escape to safety. Penelope whirled to face the dogs.

Penelope recognized the largest raccoon as the one from the watering hole. The others looked like his mate and an older offspring, perhaps a year-old son or daughter. This smallest one turned and scratched the shepherd's nose, escaping momentarily.

The raccoons leaped toward the river, putting the pigs between them and the dogs. Quietly, the large raccoon asked, "Will you help us?"

Strange, but Penelope thought it sounded almost like a challenge. She didn't look at the raccoons, though. Her gaze was fixed on the dogs just feet away from her. They were so close that she could almost smell their breath.

Dogs. Penelope couldn't let the shepherd kill the raccoons. When the fox kits were killed, she had been locked away in her sty; she had been just a piglet.

"Penelope," Santiago said, "Let's get out of here."

But Penelope shook her head. This time, she could do something.

Choose to be brave, Penelope told herself. But still, she trembled at the barks. And trembling, she charged. She butted the smallest dog, knocking it away from a raccoon. The dog snarled, whirled to meet her, and then backed away with another deep-throated growl.

"Come on!" she yelled to Santiago.

Following her lead, he charged into the fray, trampling on the dogs' soft paws with his hooves. When the dogs dodged aside, Penelope butted their soft stomachs.

Their sudden attack brought the three dogs up short.

Penelope's eyes were wide. She searched the darkness for other dogs while still tracking the three in front of her. It seemed they were alone. The odds weren't too bad, then: five against three.

Taking advantage of the confusion, though, the raccoons had scampered up a tree.

Two against three, Penelope corrected herself. She wondered if she and Santiago could make it back to the watering hole where there would be other animals to help. No, their retreat in that direction was cut off by the dogs.

The raccoons scrambled out on a branch that hung over the ferry; they dropped to the ferry's deck. A moment later, they were clearly silhouetted in the cabin's lantern light. The ferryman cast off, and with soft grunts, started poling across the river.

"Hey! You have to pay to ride that ferry," Santiago yelled.

Outrage filled Penelope. Why did the raccoons get a free ride, and they didn't?

By then the dogs had regrouped and were advancing with low growls, pulling her attention back to them. The three dogs darted forward and back, neatly cutting the pigs apart, separating them and making them fight their own battles. Two took on Santiago while one stood before Penelope.

Penelope wished she were like Santiago. He charged the shepherds while she analyzed the differences in these and the other dogs they'd met. The shepherds fought silently. Penelope almost wished for the baying of hounds, so she could pinpoint her enemy easier. Meanwhile, Santiago was slowly pushing back his two dogs, away from the river.

I can do the same, she encouraged herself. Imitating Santiago, she dashed forward, slashing with hooves while twisting frantically to avoid the dog's long, yellow teeth.

The dog whirled and nipped at her heels, but Penelope lashed out a kick with her hind leg. The dog yelped in surprise and backed away growling. Penelope squealed loudly in answer and charged again, forcing the dog to retreat toward the bushes. Santiago was also backing his dogs into the bushes.

Panting, the pigs stopped and stared at the dogs.

"The raccoons are gone," Santiago yelled. "Leave us alone!"

It was a standoff, and the lead dog was smart enough to realize this. Besides, his quarry, the raccoons, were long gone. With a last aggravated yelp, the lead dog slunk back into the shrubs. The others followed, whimpering.

Breathing hard, Penelope stood her ground. Would they return? Rain soaked her back and collected in droplets on her lashes. She shuddered, but in spite of her fear, a sense of pride filled her. Dogs would always scare her, but at least this once, she had faced them and won. If she could help it, dogs would never be cruel again. She shrugged up her shoulders trying to release tension, and then stiffly turned.

The ferry was already halfway across the great river, halfway to the wider world. They'd have to wait until tomorrow to try again. The raccoons were hanging over the back of the ferry, watching the shore. Their eyes gleamed red. One turned and held out a paw to the ferryman, who stepped forward and took something from the raccoon.

The ferry stopped midstream; the ferryman moved to the opposite side of the boat to turn it toward the pigs.

Why was he coming back?

When the boat bumped the dock, the ferryman yelled, "Hurry, then. Storm's building."

Santiago stepped aboard the heaving deck, and then turned back, ready to steady Penelope.

Penelope hesitated. If she stepped on board that ferry, her life would change forever. She looked at Santiago. "Are you sure?"

The ferryman called again, "The raccoons have paid your coins. Hurry!"

Santiago's eyes glowed in the lantern light. "Yes, Penelope. I'm sure."

She stepped onto the ferry, closed her eyes, and lifted her head, trying to feel if that one step had made her any different. No, she was still Penelope.

She opened her eyes and followed Santiago toward the cabin.

Santiago stopped to speak to the ferryman. "Thank you for coming back for us."

The ferryman shrugged, "It's my job." With that, he concentrated on his work.

When Penelope and Santiago were settled in the cabin, the raccoons approached.

The biggest one asked, "Why did you help us?"

In her mind's ear, Penelope heard old Mrs. MacDonald reciting Shakespeare: "He that is thy friend indeed, He will help thee in thy need." She called it out clear and loud, and then bowed over one rear leg.

"We thank you, lady and sir," the raccoon said. "Your hearts are gentle. Your kindness in helping us paid your way to the wider world. You're the first animals in a long time who faced the dogs and tried to help us."

The rain started pouring then, just in time to hide Penelope's blush. She understood that the raccoons had used the dogs as a sort of test, to help them decide who could board the ferry.

"You did it," Santiago whispered, "By myself, I wouldn't have done it."

"We did it," Penelope said. "You gave me courage, and you helped.

Santiago said, "That line of poetry is one for us to live by."

Penelope agreed. Their travels had been fast and hard, but in the midst, she felt they were growing and changing. Deciding to help others felt like a good decision, a wise decision. Victoria Marie would approve. Penelope echoed Santiago's words, "We will help all those in need we come across."

The ferry moved silently across the dark waters carrying them across the Mississippi River in the company of new friends. Penelope wanted to study the shore they had left behind, but she didn't allow herself to look back. Her heart thumped, while the raccoon's words repeated as a litany in her mind: If you cross, you can never return.

For better or worse, she and Santiago were going to the wider world. They could never return. Never return. Never.

6

A STRANGE PLACE

A small raccoon sat at the breakfast table, buttering toast. His shirt was blue; his vest and pants were navy; his feet were bare. Josiah Crabtree was the son of their host, Mr. Earl Crabtree, who sat at the head of the mahogany table. The raccoons were the guardians of the ferry, and, as such, the Crabtrees occupied a prominent position in Rock Island society. Their home was the newest—and largest—in Rock Island. Greek Revival architecture was sweeping the east coast, and the Crabtrees had built in the latest fashion. The white-columned house sat on a bluff, like a Greek temple, overlooking both the Rock River and, in the distance, the V where the Rock River met the Mississippi River.

The dining room was elaborate. Corinthian columns flanked a fireplace, and above the mantel hung a huge family portrait.

Josiah saw Penelope studying it. "My grandmother," he said.

"You look like her." Penelope only said it because it was expected. From the gilded frame, the old raccoon's face grimaced above a pink silk dress. Penelope didn't think the matriarch looked like Josiah or his father.

But the comment pleased Mr. Crabtree. "It's my mother. She was the first of my family to come to this world."

Penelope decided the old raccoon looked so stern because she had to wear that pink silk dress. Penelope squirmed inside her borrowed blue taffeta dress. It didn't give her room to move. Sailors need pants, she decided. After the meal, she'd ask for something more suitable.

"What is this world, exactly," Santiago asked.

"It's a parallel world, one you can only enter by certain ferries or ships in certain locations. It's called many things. The ancients called it the Mutare Fata, the place where fates can change. Natives of this land called it the Quinnipiac, the place on the river where you change course. Around here, we just call it the Land of Liberty. Or just Liberty."

Penelope liked that. A land named Liberty was just the sort of place she'd like to live her life.

"Why do you want to go to sea?" Josiah asked. He brushed toast crumbs from his clothes and helped himself to oatmeal.

"It's been my dream, our dream," Santiago said. Unlike Penelope, he looked comfortable in his clothes, as if he'd grown up wearing shirts, vests and pants.

Mr. Crabtree pointedly picked up a spoon and showed it Santiago. Then, he scooped oatmeal into his mouth. Santiago awkwardly shoved the sterling silver spoon into the cleft of his hoof. Using hooves for picking up things was hard for both pigs. With careful movements, Santiago managed to take a bite. He looked up and smiled at his host.

Mr. Crabtree beamed back. "You're learning fast."

They finished breakfast in silence, for which Penelope was grateful. She had to concentrate on using her own spoon.

Finally, Mr. Crabtree pushed back his plate and poured a cup of coffee for everyone. "This is a comfortable border town," he said. "You should settle down here. Maybe become a guardian, so you can cross back and forth. We go over a couple times a month, looking for animals like yourselves who want to come to Liberty. Not all get to cross, you know."

"Like the brown bear and possum we saw?"

"We've been watching them. But the bear is old, and the possum, well, she's always angry. We only let young, healthy intelligent creatures come to Liberty."

That policy made sense in some ways, Penelope thought. Still, it made her sad. Her parents, for example, would never get to come here.

Santiago held his cup between both hooves and took a sip. He grimaced at the bitter coffee. "We don't want to go back. How do we get to New York Harbor from here?"

Penelope had followed Josiah's lead by pouring milk and spooning sugar into her coffee. She let Santiago taste hers, and he promptly doctored his own cup.

Mr. Crabtree sighed. "I'll show you my maps."

"Maps?" Santiago set down the coffee cup and leaned forward.

"Yes, I've got several good ones. It's late fall, though. I'd recommend you stop in Philadelphia and stay there a few months. Get used to Liberty."

"We'd like to sail right away," Santiago insisted.

"Boats don't sail much in the winter anyway. You can arrive in the spring, in time to get positions on good boats. Besides, you'll need to talk to the Freedom Society. They have seed money for animals such as yourselves, to help you get a start."

"Money?"

"Yes, you'll need to learn about money."

Penelope squirmed against the uncomfortable dress. There were many things they needed to learn in this new world.

After breakfast, Mr. Crabtree led them to the library where he spread out maps on a wooden desk. Santiago eagerly hunched over them, trying to make sense of the drawings.

"Here's the Mississippi River, from New Orleans to St. Paul. We're sitting right here, at Rock Island, Illinois," Mr. Crabtree explained.

While Santiago was initiated into the mysteries of maps, Penelope sat on the upholstered seat of a bay window and gazed out at the rivers. A gleaming white paddle wheeler was turning from the Mississippi River into the Rock River. She watched in awe as it chugged upstream, steam billowing. It moved so fast. Could sailboats go faster?

Mr. Crabtree noticed the paddle wheeler, too. "We get steam boat traffic almost every day now. You could stay here and make a good living on the riverboats."

Penelope and Santiago looked at each other.

It was tempting, Penelope thought. They had come so far, and maybe they should stop here and be content with this corner of Liberty. Moving on meant more risks; but she wanted to see the whole world, not just the Mississippi River from New Orleans to St. Paul. She shook her head slightly.

Santiago nodded back, then said to Mr. Crabtree, "No. We're going to sea."

"Foolish, if you ask me," Mr. Crabtree said. "Steamboats, not sailboats, are the future."

Santiago ignored the comment. "Do you have maps of the whole world?"

When the raccoon showed him a globe, Santiago was entranced. He spun the globe, watching the lands go around and around. Then, he closed his eyes, stopped the globe and pointed. "Please tell us about this place."

The game engrossed everyone for hours, as Mr. Crabtree told about Japan, the Indian Sea, the southern polar continent—Wilkes' Land, it was called, after the famous explorer.

Adventure. Penelope whispered the word to herself. It was everywhere in Liberty. She thought about what Mr. Crabtree had said: Not every animal gets to cross.

They had done the impossible by escaping the farm with its threat of pigs becoming bacon. But what were they do to now? No other family member would ever come here—unless Runt made it. That fact alone made her uneasy about thinking of taking the easy way out, the first option they saw. For the sake of those left behind, she couldn't live a small life. Mr. Crabtree had considered them important enough to bring over to Liberty, and she would imitate his attitude. There would be no little people—animal or human—and no little places.

They stayed a week with the Crabtrees, studying maps and getting used to the sight of intelligent animals standing upright, talking, conducting business with human and animal. The dogs, especially, startled Penelope at first. But every one she met was courteous and soft-spoken. Perhaps intelligent dogs were all kind instead of cruel.

They met with the Freedom Committee who provided seed money for creatures coming into Liberty. The director of the local committee was Mrs. Newcombe, a large woman who wore huge bonnets and wide hooped skirts. Penelope endured several hours of lecturing about the latest clothing fashions before flatly refusing to try on a hoop skirt. Only afterwards did the wonder of talking with a human occur to her, but Liberty freely mixed humans and creatures, and it just seemed natural.

With money from the Freedom Committee, Santiago bought his first map. More practical, Penelope chose a set of clothes for each of them. She compromised with a cotton split-skirt which she would wear until they reached the sea. But she insisted on a piece of traditional sailor clothing for each: a black pea coat. A few meager supplies for their trip eastward finished their shopping. By the end of the week, they were ready to head east.

"Some day soon," Josiah Crabtree said, "I'll put in a train line from Chicago to here. It'll be the first rail line to the Mississippi River. I'll put Rock Island on the map."

Even as she wondered what the train would look like, Penelope had no doubt Josiah would do exactly that. For now, though, they had no choice but to climb into a coach for a bumpy ride to Chicago. The ornate yellow and gold coach was pulled by a family of intelligent horses who made their living running the coach lines.

Because they had just arrived in Liberty, the horses allowed them both to travel for the price of one. The mare taking fares shrugged off their thanks. "Pass it on by helping someone else when you can."

"We will," Penelope agreed.

When they were safely settled in the coach, Santiago pulled out his new map and traced their route for Penelope. They had to cross six states—Illinois, Indiana, Ohio, Pennsylvania, New Jersey, and New York—before they would finally reach New York Harbor. It would be a long journey.

Still, they were young and free, and they were in the midst of their own adventure.

They traveled steadily. With new sights and new ways of doing things greeting them daily, they depended on each other even more. Penelope remained cheerful despite hunger, bad weather, or small injuries. At dark moments, she recalled a line of Mrs. McDonald's poetry to cheer their hearts. For his part, Santiago always made friends with other travelers. They learned much about the customs and history of Liberty through many a congenial conversation.

In Chicago, they climbed aboard the noisy, smelly train, and they came finally to Philadelphia, the City of Brotherly Love. Here, they lingered through the late fall and winter, getting their bearings in Liberty. During the day, they both worked for Mr. Skype, a stooped black man who wore a monocle, a single eyepiece, in his left eye. Mr. Skype's produce store was successful because it brought in fresh vegetables from the countryside; in Liberty, everyone was vegetarian. The store's back room became their home. Mr. Skype deducted the cost of the room from their pay.

Even so, Santiago managed to save a mite each week. "For our own boat," he said. He kept a leather purse beneath their mattress and counted it once a week, smiling in satisfaction at how the pile of coins grew.

At night, they went to Portico Row to one of the brick and marble row mansions where they struggled to learn letters and numbers with Mrs. Mellie, the widowed Siamese cat schoolmarm. While they enjoyed their lessons, the best part was Mr. Purtle, her butler, who was an old box turtle. He owned a small sailing dinghy, and on nice days, he took them out on the Delaware River. They struggled to learn how to furl and unfurl sails; the hardest was furling, or rolling sails up smoothly. Then Mr. Purtle turned the Duke Luke into the wind, and they struggled to learn how to tack—zigzag back and forth—to make headway in the white-tipped waves of winter. It was a gentle beginning to their education as sailors.

They spent long evenings listening to Miss Mellie's stories of her hometown, Boston. It was a sailing town, and to prove it, she had stories about captains, packets to China, speed records, and—most of all—shipwrecks.

"That's how I lost my dear husband, the late Mr. Mellie," Mrs. Mellie sighed. "He was a fine-looking rat, and a fine sea captain, too. But a wretched sea serpent wrecked his ship."

Penelope and Santiago learned everything they could from Mrs. Mellie's stories.

By late winter, Mr. Purtle sent them out on their own for long, glorious days with their faces in the wind.

Penelope and Santiago were together, they were learning to sail, and they were content. Still, when the first robin returned to the north, Penelope said, "Soon."

And Santiago agreed. "Boston Harbor, then, instead of New York Harbor?"

"Yes," Penelope said.

Before they left in early March, Mr. Skype went through the store and helped them pick out sturdy gear and clothing suitable for Boston society. "If you want to get ahead in the world," he said, "you need to dress right."

In her backpack, Penelope carried a book of poems and a journal in which to write her own poems. Santiago had his purse of coins, a book of maps and a journal in which to draw his own maps.

Thus they came, at last, in the early spring, to the Boston Harbor, the home of the tall ships. The harbor was fringed with the bright yellow-green of spring, and a sea breeze tickled the Talbert's noses. But it was the acres of canvas sails that caught their eyes and their imagination. A brisk wind blew the Union Jack or Stars and Stripes straight out, while departing ships unfurled sails, and incoming ships furled them, making it a place swarming with activity: seagulls dipped, horse-drawn carts and wagons loaded or unloaded at long wharves, and everywhere, to and fro, there moved men and intelligent animals on important business.

Penelope and Santiago looked at each other with delight. By evening, surely, they would have a berth on an outgoing sailing ship.

7

BOSTON

Boston Harbor was created by the deep waters where the Charles River and Mystic River spilled out into the sea; the depth allowed ocean-going ships to dock and unload their wares. In Boston itself, the wharves arched out into the harbor. At the north end, the Charles River Bridge connected Boston with Charlestown and Bunker Hill, which rose above the town. Wharves jutted into the Charles River. Curving around on the Boston side, the oldest and biggest wharves were at the eastern end. Long Wharf—half a mile long, built in 1710—and India Wharf—built in 1807—boasted large counting houses. The bottom floors held offices and display rooms where merchants could view goods just arriving. Upstairs were the actual auction houses. Here, offices humming with secretaries who clacked out letters on typewriters or added up accounts on adding machines. If a sailing ship was a queen bee, here were the drones that kept her healthy. Toward the south end of the harbor, the wharves were smaller and serviced smaller ships.

"This is it!" Penelope struggled to keep her hooves still as they stepped onto the first wooden wharf. Clip-clip-clip-clop.

Fortunately, the nervous clatter was lost in the general hubbub.

Penelope and Santiago didn't have even a fourth of what they needed to buy their own boat. Even if they had saved enough money, they agreed that they needed experience under a good captain before they would sail by themselves. So, they hopefully worked their way up and down each wharf, stopping at every ship on the south side of Boston Harbor and asking if it needed two sailors.

"Aloft, you wouldn't last an hour," said Captain Eznick, a large orangutan with long fingers and toes. He commanded the *Cormorant*, a sleek sloop with triangular, lanteen sails. Penelope longed to climb into the rigging, but the First Mate hustled them down the gangplank before she could suggest a trial.

"Never had a pig as a crewman before," said Captain Brice, a short stocky Irish woman who spoke with a heavy accent. Hers was a square sailed schooner, the *Endurance*, but it was small, and her crew numbered only eight. "Well, I can take one of you, that's all."

But Penelope and Santiago had vowed to go to sea together. They tried their luck at the next boat. And the next. No one, it seemed, wanted two pigs as crewmen.

Finally, at dusk, they came to the middle of the harbor at the eastern end of the semicircle of wharves. From this vantage point they could see the shore curving off in both directions. Commercial Street ran around the harbor, echoing the contours of the land. Here were two- or three-story buildings, mostly brick or wood, with colorful carved and painted signs hanging before doorways. Lantern light from those being lit just now reflected off the dark water. Spicy smells spilled from tavern doorways, along with laughter and song.

"We need a place to sleep." Penelope hurt all over; her jaws ached from talking so much, trying to convince some ship captain to take them on; her leg muscles were tight, aching with a longing to climb rigging, any rigging, on any ship; her eyes burned from all the bright white canvas and unshed tears of frustration. "Tomorrow we'll talk to the rest." She waved at the north side of the harbor. Breathing deeply of the salt air, Penelope studied the boats docked there. *Will we find a position tomorrow?* Hope mingled with nervousness. *Soon*, she whispered to cheer herself, *we'll go to sea.*

They strolled along Commercial Street, watching for signs of inns. At the Tea Party Inn, they asked about rooms, but they were expensive here on the waterfront. The Talberts had watched their money carefully but had little left except the leather purse with their boat money, and Santiago had vowed not to spend that. The innkeeper, a cheerful man with tattooed arms, suggested, "Try down some side streets."

As they trudged down Lime Alley toward Charter Street, suddenly Santiago tapped Penelope's shoulder. "Look. This way," he said, and hurried Penelope across the street and along a bit until he stopped in front of a small shop whose sign read, "Maps. Cricket Mansfield, Proprietor." In a clean, brightly lit window was a smaller sign: Help Wanted.

Eagerly, Santiago pushed open the door, and they walked inside. Directly ahead, Penelope saw a wooden box holding upright rolls of yellowed maps; indeed, similar boxes were crowded in tight groups throughout the room. To the right, though, was a viewing wall where maps could be tacked up and studied. Right now, it was covered with a three-foot square map of Boston itself. Lanterns hung at either side of the wall, casting a warm glow on the oiled paper. Santiago stood with his forelegs behind his back and leaned forward so his white snout was just inches from the surface.

"Look," Santiago waved at the map. "The penmanship. The scale. The colors. The lines."

Even to Penelope, the map looked like the work of a master.

Santiago bent to look closely. "Is it signed? Who made this map?"

From the opposite corner, a voice piped up. "Cricket Mansfield, at your service."

Leaving her drafting desk, a slight Oriental woman wove her way through the boxes of maps and bowed before Penelope and Santiago. Liberty was full of such surprises that Penelope had almost expected a real cricket instead of this tiny woman.

"You are new to the city and need a map?" the woman asked.

"This is magnificent," Santiago said. "How much?"

Cricket Mansfield gave the Talberts an appraising look. "Too much for your taste."

"How much?" Santiago insisted.

"$50."

Santiago looked at Penelope helplessly, and then gestured at the map again. "I've never seen the like."

"Nor likely to, either," Cricket Mansfield said with a British accent. "I learned my trade at my father's knees, and he was the best cartographer, or map maker, in China. I sailed the South Seas and learned how the Polynesians navigate. I charted the currents of the Arctic Ocean before I went to Oxford, England to consult with the Royal Cartographer's Association." She spread out tiny, ink-stained hands. "My maps are the best in the world."

Santiago's eyes shone bright with envy. "What kind of ink did you use here? Where did you get such fine paper?"

Cricket's eyebrows shot up. "Ah, you're a map maker?"

She unpinned the map and laid it out on her drafting desk and for the next hour, she and Santiago were engrossed in mapmaking. Penelope amused herself by looking randomly through the maps. When she found an interesting one, she took it to the viewing wall and tacked it up. After sorting through several dozen bins, she saw something folded up, lying in the bottom of one. It was a ragged, ancient map, badly colored and lettered, but with strange islands dotting the Atlantic. She pinned it to the wall and studied it. The mapmaker had drawn strange creatures, whose coils and scales dipped and hid amidst the islands. Around one island had been written, "Here be Sea Serpents."

Hideous beasts. Here in Liberty, she had met many intelligent dogs and was slowly learning to accept them without fear. It seemed to her that sea serpents were the wolves of the sea and would be far worse than the hounds back home. It wasn't necessarily the killing that bothered her because that was the way of nature. It was the cruelty that scared her, angered her. Penelope shivered. She could imagine sea serpents toying with a victim before killing it. Quickly, Penelope took the map down, re-folded it, and replaced it at the bottom of the bin, as if she could escape the fear by hiding the map.

Finally, grouchy and tired and hungry, she stomped over to the drafting table. "Santiago, my stomach is growling."

He looked up, eyes bright, ears perky. "What? Oh." He blinked. "I'm hungry, too, I guess."

Cricket's long braid had fallen over her shoulder and lay in dark loops on the map in front of her. She straightened up and flipped it to her back, where it hung to her knees. "Right. You can start in the morning. I've a room—tiny, but clean—that I'll throw in with your wages."

She reached over and removed the "Help Wanted" sign from the window.

Santiago blinked, not understanding. But Penelope saw immediately that Cricket was right. Before they could take off to sea, Santiago needed to learn mapmaking. She sighed. It probably meant a year's delay, but without it, Santiago would never be content. "We'll take it," she said. At *least*, she thought, *they were in Boston*. While Santiago learned mapmaking, she would study the seafaring world, too.

And so, the summer and fall passed. Santiago barely noticed the seasons changing, but Penelope chafed at the wait. Yes, she grudgingly admitted, it was time well spent even though she resented each day spent on land.

While Santiago sat day after day at the drafting table, Penelope put on sailor's dungarees and picked up odd jobs. Her first job was as a stevedore, unloading goods brought from

India by the East India Shipping Company on the Mermaid. The receiving officer in charge was Evelyn Russet, a large poodle. Her long black hair was twisted into curls, much like the dreadlocks of the humans from Jamaica.

"We're bred to be water dogs," Evelyn said proudly. "My hair sheds water as well as any polar bear's fur."

The work was hard, lifting heavy boxes of goods and passing them along a line of workers, stretching from the deep hold up to the deck and then off the ship to the dock. The last in line loaded the box onto a wagon to be taken to the counting house. Sometimes she caught a whiff of a pungent herb or spice. Penelope liked to guess at the contents of these boxes: cinnamon, curry, and black pepper.

She worked hard, so the other stevedores accepted her easily. This meant that whenever there was a new ship to unload, someone sent a message to let her know; she was kept busy loading and unloading goods from around the world. It was good work, but it made her want to go to sea even more.

On weekends, she helped the tattooed cook at the Tea Party Inn. Fish was a favorite food in Boston Harbor, either grilled or in stews; everyone agreed that fish with scales weren't intelligent creatures, so it was fine to eat them. While she cooked or served, Penelope listened to the captains gossiping, so that, within a month or two, she knew which boats had good captains and which had cruel ones. She was glad they hadn't signed on with Captain Brice. The wild Irishwoman had a reputation as a miser; they said she never lost a crewman, never lost a cargo, and never let a penny escape her tight fist.

After work, the Talberts lingered in the tavern, where Penelope fell in love with sea shanties; something about the beat or the work-rhythm of the songs fell pleasantly on her ear.

"Hey-lee!"

"Ho-lip!"

"Wey-hey!"

"Yo-heave-yo!"

She was almost embarrassed to write a sea shanty in her poetry journal, but soon it was brimming with them, and she had to start a second journal.

For his part, Santiago was in heaven, learning everything he could from Cricket Mansfield.

"Slow down," she often told him. "Take the time to do it well."

"But time is so short; when we finally go to sea, I'll have time to practice then."

"Oh, ho! You think a sailor's life is a life of leisure?"

"No, but—"

"Then, start this map again. Your lines are too crooked."

And in spite of his complaining, Santiago was glad of a master who held him to a high standard.

At night, he was full of new information to share with Penelope. "Did you know," he asked her, "there aren't just seven seas to sail? There are 54." He named them, then promised, "We'll sail them all."

One day, he showed her a new book, *Wind and Current Charts* by Lt. Maury, a Navy man. Maury had worked for several years compiling information from thousands of Navy log books. The result were the most accurate charts ever seen that showed currents and winds for seas across the world. Previous charts had just shown major currents or winds; these showed details such as minor variations within the Gulf Stream, one of the major currents in the Atlantic.

"It's like they've been sailing blind," Santiago said. "With these new charts, sailing will be faster and faster, as captains take easier routes."

"Do the captains realize this?"

"No, but they will. Cricket is putting this information into her new maps. It's a great time for me to be learning mapmaking, just as these new charts are coming through."

At odd times, they snuck away to sail on borrowed or rented boats—always using the new charts. Sometimes they managed short one- or two-day runs, and once, in Cricket's yacht, they sailed for a week up to a farm in Maine. The Hilldebrands, a family of rabbits, was especially good at making fine papers for her maps; Cricket made trips to their farm every year to inspect and order new papers. The pigs' skills in handling any size sailboat were growing.

Deep winter was a time when ships stayed home, and there was little work on the wharves. The icehouses still had plenty of work, said the other stevedores. Penelope heard this was back breaking work. She might've taken it easy for the coldest months, but she was handing over too much money to Cricket.

It started their first week at the map shop. Cricket bought an old map from a sailor needing money; she showed it first to Penelope. Not sure if she was repelled or fascinated by the sea serpent it showed, Penelope bought it.

"Crazy," Santiago said. "We could save that money for our boat. Besides, I could draw one better than that."

That wasn't the point. This one was old, even Cricket said so. After that, Cricket secretly showed any map with sea serpents to Penelope, and she bought every one. Her repulsion had turned to passion. She wanted to know more about sea serpents. No, she wanted to know everything about sea serpents. She let it be known along the wharves and taverns that anyone who had a tale about a sea serpent would find her a good audience. Many a strange crewman sought her out to tell his wild tale. In the fall, she started a new journal in which she wrote sea serpent stories; that winter she filled another. She decided one thing: she never wanted to meet a sea serpent. The maps would show her places to avoid.

When Santiago worked late downstairs in the map shop—which was more often than she liked—and she had nothing to do, Penelope rolled out map after map onto their bed and studied the fantastic, grotesque, hideously beautiful creatures. They were all drawn differently, except the coils; they all had coils, long snake-like coils. All these extra maps took extra money. Especially if she wanted to keep her collection a secret from Santiago, who thought it foolish.

One day in early January, a sleety rain started in the early morning, coating everything with a half inch of ice; by evening, the storm whipped into a blinding snow. When it stopped at midnight, the ice was hidden beneath a six inch layer of snow, a deceptive blanket which smoothed out bumps and holes. Those few who ventured out the next day blundered across treacherous roads. No one worked that day, but after two more nights of hard freezes, Evelyn, the poodle, sent word that the icemen should report the next morning. Penelope decided to give it a try; if she could do the heavy work of a stevedore, then she could be an iceman.

8

THE ICE KING

Penelope rose while it was still dark and dressed for the cold. She put on dungarees, then oilcloth dungarees over that. The stevedores warned her that cutting ice was wet, as well as cold, work. She added three shirts, then buttoned on her wool pea coat and jammed a black tarpaulin hat over her ears. She trotted carefully through the dark, silent streets. It was an hour before dawn when she met up with the other stevedores at the Charles River Bridge and climbed onto sleds pulled by roan Belgian draft horses.

"How far?" Penelope asked the lead horse.

His hooves were almost hidden beneath shaggy dark hair, or feathering, on his lower legs. Belgians usually didn't have such feathering, so he must have a Clydesdale or Shire mother. He was a huge young stallion who wore blinders to keep him looking straight, so he wouldn't get distracted from the job. He had to turn his head almost all the way around to look at Penelope. "Two miles to Fresh Pond. They say the ice is fourteen inches thick." His voice was deep and strong, and the words made white puffs in the frigid air. "It'll be a hard day's work, but the Ice King pays well."

"As long as you don't get cross winds of him," said the horse behind him. From their looks, Penelope guessed the second stallion was the young one's father. He was probably harnessed second to steady the young one's high spirits and keep him working hard.

By the time they were out of town, the sun glittered on ice-encrusted tree limbs. It was a hard, brittle world, where things snapped easily. Everywhere, broken limbs littered the ground. Here and there, entire trees were toppled and uprooted from the weight of ice.

Halfway to Fresh Pond, a sleigh passed them. Six black horses pulled it, so it went at a fast clip, bells jangling in the clear air. It passed so quickly, Penelope couldn't see the passengers. When they arrived at the Pond, the sleigh was already there. Dawn was streaking the eastern sky with soft shades of lilac.

A large wooden table sat on a sliver of land that jutted out toward the frozen pond. Covered with a linen tablecloth trimmed in lace, the table was full of covered silver dishes. A polar bear seated himself in the only chair.

At Penelope's questioning gaze, the young stallion whickered softly, "The Ice King, Captain Kingsley. And Frenchie, his first mate."

Captain Kingsley was a massive polar bear, yellow-white fur gleaming against the carved chair. He wore a vest, but little else; his own natural fur was warmer than any clothing he might try to wear. One eye was covered with a black patch, but the other eye was a dull black that absorbed all light.

He was attended by an Emperor Penguin who sported a French beret. He was large as far as penguins go, but next to Captain Kingsley, he was dwarfed. His belly was white; his back, black. The only color was the orangish-yellow on the sides of his head and an orange streak down his pointed beak. Even when his head drooped like a flower too heavy for its stalk, the penguin still looked like he was standing at attention.

He removed the cover of a silver bowl and offered the boiled potatoes, turnips and carrots for Captain Kingsley's inspection. The polar bear nodded, and Frenchie piled vegetables onto Captain Kingsley's plate. This was followed by three fat grilled trout. Using the finest of silverware, Captain Kingsley ate.

Now Penelope noticed a porcupine poking at pots and pans over a roaring fire. The scent of cinnamon apples made her stomach growl. She had grabbed only a crust of bread before coming out—obviously, a mistake.

Captain Kingsley ate for fifteen minutes, devouring everything placed in front of him. He remained oblivious to his surroundings, despite a bustle of noise as the workers sorted themselves into experienced and inexperienced icemen. Finally, Captain Kingsley pushed back his china. He stretched, his arms reaching toward the glittery trees; his paws alone were as large as Penelope's head. He yawned. His mouth was spacious enough to swallow a piglet whole.

Penelope shivered in the pale winter morning. She had feared—or admired—the choice of words didn't matter, they were almost the same emotion—Farmer MacDonald because he controlled everything on the farm. She had feared the hound's long, yellow teeth. She had feared where the red wagon might take her. She had feared the shepherd dogs that almost prevented their crossing to Liberty. But the polar bears' easy, supple movements made her acutely aware of his strength; she learned admiration—and fear—anew.

The polar bear finally stood and became the Ice King, hard and brittle. Penelope realized he did everything with complete concentration. While he had picnicked, the ice operation hadn't existed; he was a polar bear enjoying a good breakfast on a frigid day. Now, he was the Ice King, the head of a vast operation that provided ice year-round to far-flung places. Many had thought his scheme of selling ice to the tropics was mad; he had fought against all naysayers and created a thriving trade in frozen water. And there was ice to harvest.

"No mistakes this morning," the Ice King bellowed. "We need 300 tons of ice for each brig we send out, and I'm increasing the fleet this year."

He motioned to a short woman to step forward. "This is Captain Brice. She'll take charge of the *Hallowe'en*, the newest ship of our fleet. She's here to observe the ice cutting operation."

A stevedore next to Penelope said, "She's never lost a crewman to storms or dangers or carelessness. Never."

Penelope nodded. "I've heard." Maybe it didn't matter so much that Captain Brice was stingy with her pay; a perfect safety record was indeed rare.

Captain Brice wore her curly hair short, tucked up under her captain's hat. She said nothing but nodded easily to the icemen. A few nodded back, but mostly they didn't care who took care of the ice once it was packed into the icehouses.

Captain Kingsley called, "Let's get busy. We have five icehouses to fill before the weather changes."

Frenchie said, "Sydney, Calcutta, Bombay, Rio de Janeiro—zey all want ice from zee Fresh Pond. No other ice will do."

Captain Brice disappeared in the crowd again, but Penelope realized Captain Kingsley's introduction essentially gave Captain Brice permission to wander all over the pond to observe operations.

Under Captain Kingsley's one-eyed stare, the workers scattered to start the tedious process: scraping snow from the ice, marking out eighteen inch blocks and then sawing with one or two-man ice saws.

Penelope tucked a huge snow shovel under her arms and scraped snow, exposing clear, solid ice. It was easy work for an hour, tedious for the second hour and exhausting for the third. She didn't get to rest until after the fourth impossible hour, when they had a short break for lunch of hot thick stew and bitter coffee. The icemen crowded around the bonfire and ate greedily. One bowl barely filled her empty stomach, so, fortunately, there was plenty for seconds and thirds. While she ate, Penelope thought enviously of Santiago huddled over a table and drawing maps with a hot water bottle to keep his hooves warm. She was ready to be at sea, not doing a landlubber's job.

Penelope finally quieted her stomach's grumblings, then dropped her bowl in the cauldron of hot water to be washed. She wandered toward the Pond, looking at the two sleds piled with ice columns, 50 foot long by 18 inches wide. After lunch, the horses would start the long pull back toward town; the remaining sleds would be loaded before nightfall. At the icehouses, the columns would be split into 18-inch cubes before they were packed in pine straw.

The pond had dark slashes of open water. Carefully, Penelope stepped onto the ice and walked out a dozen feet. She leaned over and peered at the stark reflections of bare trees.

Crack! Penelope jerked upright. She was standing on the outer strip of ice, and now she saw it had been partially cut away from the main ice mass. Carefully, she stepped backward. Crack! The sharp report made everyone on shore turn toward her.

"No!" The Ice King bellowed. "Get off there!"

Before Penelope could take another step, the ice split away raggedly, breaking where it hadn't yet been sawed. It floated free. Penelope waved her forelegs, trying to maintain her balance, but with water splashing over it, the ice was suddenly slippery. She slipped easily, silently, into the dark water.

Cold. The wool pea coat was heavy, waterlogged, pulling Penelope deeper. She struggled to unbutton it, but her hooves couldn't work it. She kicked upward, but the coat dragged her down.

Did sailors know how to swim? Why had she never learned?

Cold. Her thinking was already slower from the cold, somehow she knew that. But it was the hat that concerned her the most. Sailors wore black tarpaulin hats, canvas hats that were soaked with tar to make them waterproof. But her hat was lost in the dark swirling water.

Cold. She needed to breathe. Sailors breathed air, not water. Kick. Kick. Above was a brighter area, where the ice had been taken out. The oilcloth shirts under the pea coat felt crinkly as she struggled toward the light.

A dark shape covered the light.

Cold. Massive paws shoved under her forelegs and hauled her upward. Tossed her onto the main ice mass. Penelope looked up into Captain Kingsley's eyes.

His eye patch had been torn away in his dive to save her, and she saw it had covered a sightless black eye that was twisted to always look upward. His other black eye studied her with fury. "Foolish pig! What were you doing so close to the edge?"

Then, the porcupine cook was there to strip off her clothes, and three stevedores carried her to a pallet beside the roaring fire. Penelope saw Captain Kingsley shake like a dog and realized he was almost dry already. But she was still cold, her teeth chattering uncontrollably.

A few minutes later, she heard jangling. She was picked up again and laid across the front seat of a sleigh.

The porcupine threw warm blankets over her, and then placed hot water bottles around her. He tut-tutted and spoke to himself: "The boss hates it when this happens. Blames himself. He'll be mad for a week."

Wearily, she thought that he must have done this before—he was prepared. Captain Kingsley climbed into the back seat and watched her, as the horses raced toward town. Apparently, like Captain Brice, Kingsley was proud of his record of never losing a sailor—or iceman.

She woke in her own bed over Cricket's house. Later, Santiago told her Captain Kingsley had brought her home and carried her upstairs himself and tucked her into bed.

"You worried me," Santiago murmured. He held another spoonful of vegetable broth to Penelope's mouth. She let the warmth spread through her, then slept.

Santiago was there each time Penelope opened her eyes. Toward evening, Penelope woke from yet another nap, and this time, she was hungry. She ate three boiled potatoes.

Quietly, Santiago said, "You scared me."

She studied his face. The white forehead blaze was wrinkled with worry, and the rest of his face looked even blacker than usual. "We've been too busy lately."

"Yes," he agreed. "And we'll likely get busy again, so that we don't have time to talk. Once we start to sail, we'll have very little private time, you know. But underneath everything I do, you are there."

About his emotions, Santiago was a pig of few words, so these words touched Penelope. "I understand. We need training and experience, and during this time, our jobs may take us different directions. But when we buy our own boat, our partnership will be stronger because of the different things we're learning now."

"I'm glad you understand." He touched her hoof and sighed. "Don't scare me again."

"I'll be more careful," Penelope promised.

And they talked and talked, all night, as they hadn't done since those early days back in the pig's sty.

After two days of rest, Penelope regained her strength. She keenly felt the debt she owed to Captain Kingsley; she had to find a way to repay his kindness. What would please him? The whole experience left her with a cold commitment to Captain Kingsley. On the third day after the accident, she reported back to work for the Ice King.

This time she was more cautious and soon learned every job in the ice operations. She worked her way up to a sawyer of ice within a month. It was good money, but she also enjoyed watching the Ice King work. In many ways, Captain Kingsley was like Cricket, even though their bodies were opposite: both were superb at managing their businesses.

The other stevedores disliked Captain Kingsley because he drove them hard. Penelope, though, worked willingly, driving herself even harder, in an effort to please the Captain. And he noticed.

When the weather warmed, Penelope crossed the Charles River Bridge to help load the ice brigs at Gray's Wharf. Captain Kingsley remembered her from the ice cutting crew and set her as a foreman of a loading crew. They loaded 300 tons of ice a day, working three or four days straight, packing the ice blocks in pine straw. A third of it would melt on the 70-day journey to Calcutta, India, but profits would still be huge.

After all, nature provided the ice free. All they had to do was ship it.

The second week of loading, Penelope was excited to be in charge of loading ice onto the *Hallowe'en*, the newest ship in the fleet. She was a tall, triple master with the sleeker hull design of clipper ships—a beauty! And she was promised to Captain Brice.

Penelope worked her crew hard, and they finished packing the hull tight with ice and pine straw by the end of the third day. She was tired and covered in pine straw, which made her itch and sneeze.

It was already an hour past dusk when they loaded the last ice block.

"Go on. Take off," she told her crew.

As foreman, it was her job to do a final check of the last layer of pine straw and take care of any problems. Besides, Santiago would be working on his masterpiece map—the one of the whole world showing the currents from Lt. Maury's charts. He wouldn't miss her for another hour or so.

She worked silently, efficiently, making sure the pine straw was evenly distributed. The ice compartments were dark and cool. Working as a stevedore for the last year had given her an intimate knowledge of the insides of boats, so she was working mostly by feel. She didn't light a lantern. She finished the rear compartments quickly, and then moved to the last one in the forward part of the hull. She heard voices, but kept working. Slowly, the voices came closer, louder, and more distinct.

"It's cool down 'ere," Frenchie said with satisfaction in his voice.

Captain Kingsley cleared his throat. "I'm taking this command of the *Hallowe'en*."

"What about Captain Brice? Zhe won't be happy. "

"I'll deal with her. We'll deliver this shipment."

"Why? I zought we were staying in Boston zis year."

Penelope was embarrassed she was accidentally eavesdropping. She hoped they'd just glance around and leave her to her work.

Captain Kingsley's voice went deep with longing. "I want my collection. All of it."

Frenchie was silent. The lantern in his hand swung lightly, casting a shifting shadow. "Zat means visiting every ice 'ouse. Rio de Janeiro, Sydney, Calcutta, Bombay—"

"Yes. Every single one."

"Is zat wise? Few would understand what we've done."

"I don't care. I want it all together." Captain Kingsley lifted the eye patch and rubbed his blind eye, a childish gesture that made him look tired.

"You're still dreaming about it." It wasn't a question.

Was the Captain not sleeping well? Penelope wondered.

Captain Kingsley replaced the eye patch. "We only lack one thing, and I dream of that."

"No," Frenchie shook his head. "Zat's not what you dream of."

Up to now, Captain Kingsley was just the Ice King, the hard-nosed businessman. Or the excellent swimmer who saved her. This strange conversation revealed him more as a person. There were depths to the Captain that people barely guessed at, and Frenchie understood those depths. Penelope was fascinated by the relationship. Trying to see the expressions on their faces, she straightened and bumped into the low roof.

Frenchie spun around and held up the lantern. "You! What are you doing here?"

"My job. Spreading the last layer of pine straw," Penelope managed to say calmly. "Making sure it's all done right."

Frenchie frowned. "I will do ze inspection. You may go."

"Yes, sir."

What collection did Captain Kingsley have? Why wouldn't others understand it? Penelope felt an uneasiness touch her, and she shivered. The dark hold had been comforting a moment ago, but now she hurried upward toward the lanterns on deck. Captain Kingsley, the Ice King, had deep secrets, and she hoped she'd never find out about them.

9

SEA MONSTER MAPS

One spring day, Penelope woke early and threw open the shutters to find not a cloud in the sky. Laughing, she called out a line from one of Mrs. McDonald's favorite poems by Rosetti:

"I strain my heart, I stretch my hands,
And catch at hope."

Santiago didn't share her good humor: "We should be at sea."

"No," Penelope said. "None of the ships in harbor are right for us." Leaning out the window and staring down Lime Alley to the harbor, she mentally ticked off the captains and crew of each ship. She had loaded or unloaded for most of them this past year, and had listened to their tales later in the taverns.

Santiago came to stand in the window's breeze with her. "I've learned enough about mapping. Smell that salt air! It's April."

The biggest problem was that they wanted adventure, not commerce. None of the ships in harbor offered more than a commercial run to Bermuda and back, or to England and back, or to India and back, or to Australia and back. Working as a stevedore had taught Penelope that much of shipping was boring business: delivery of goods as fast as possible. But shipping could be an adventure. Vast areas of the ocean were unexplored, as Santiago's and Cricket's maps proved. In the end, it was the maps that mattered; Penelope and Santiago could spend a lifetime filling in the blanks.

"Be patient," Penelope said.

"One more month, then. After that—"

"We'll take the first ship that seems even halfway likely," Penelope agreed.

Downstairs, the bell that hung over the door rang sweetly. Santiago and Penelope climbed down the steep stairs and then stopped short. The shop looked like a whale had beached itself on a tiny sand bar; Captain Kingsley sat on a bare strip of floor in front of the viewing wall. Even at that, he had to stoop not to hit his head on the ceiling. Frenchie, beret under his wing, perched on a stool beside him.

Cricket, herself dwarfed by the Captain, stood beside the viewing wall, with rolled up maps under her arms. She wore her best red silk jacket, so he must have sent a messenger ahead to announce his intentions to visit the shop.

"Your shop is known for its sea serpent maps," Captain Kingsley said. "I was told to talk with Santiago."

"Santiago?" Penelope turned to him in surprise.

But Santiago scooted around to the drafting table and sat where he could watch Cricket and the Captain. Penelope couldn't catch his eye. That meant Santiago was up to something, for sure. She scooted around to sit beside him.

"I'm the proprietor here," Cricket said. Her mouth was tight, which meant she was mad. "I can help you. We have many maps of the Bermuda Triangle, where sea serpents are rumored to live."

Penelope felt uneasy. She felt like she was watching a chess match, and she wasn't sure Santiago and Cricket were on the same side.

Why was Captain Kingsley so interested in sea serpents? After hours of collecting sea serpent stories, she felt rather like her territory was being invaded.

Captain Kingsley sat patiently for half an hour as Cricket unrolled map after map of the Bermuda Islands, the Caribbean, the Atlantic currents, the Gulf Stream, the Sargasso Sea, or anything remotely close to that area.

Finally, she ran out of maps. "Captain, does anything here strike your fancy?"

She must be nervous, Penelope thought. Her British accent was more pronounced than usual.

Captain Kingsley's good eye blinked. "No. Not one had a sea serpent on it. Where are they? I've heard rumors you have several very old sea serpent maps." His voice was calm, quiet. He hunched his shoulders and held his massive paws too still. Penelope shivered.

Cricket turned back to the wall and reached to unpin the map that was displayed. Her hand quivered.

Penelope opened her mouth, and then shut it.

It was Santiago who saved them.

Coming forward, he said, "Yes, Captain, we did have such a map. In fact, we've had seven maps with serpents come through the shop in the last year. Three, we sold to Captain Asad of the *Krakatoa*. You wouldn't want them anyway."

Captain Kingsley swung around to stare at Santiago. The Berkshire pig was now three years old and in his prime. He was solidly built, as you'd expect from a pig, but agile, intelligent, bright-eyed. He met Captain Kingsley's stare without flinching.

"And you are?"

"Santiago Talbert, at your service." He bowed gracefully over his extended leg.

The shop window was a bright square now, so bright Penelope couldn't see out. It made her feel like they were all locked inside a dark cave. Captain Kingsley, Frenchie, Santiago, Cricket—everyone was studying the chessboard, planning a strategy. Cricket had the secret of Penelope's sea serpent maps to protect. But why was Santiago squinting so much? Why was Captain Kingsley, and even Frenchie, so alert?

"Ah. At last. Why wouldn't I want those three maps?" Captain Kingsley asked.

"Because the sea serpents on those maps were just decorations," Santiago said.

"And you know zis, because?" In spite of being an Emperor penguin from the Antarctic, Frenchie spoke with a heavy French accent that made Penelope wonder about his background. On the dockside, it had seemed just a part of the scenery, but here in the shop, it was odd.

Santiago brushed aside the question with a gesture of his foreleg. "Mapmakers know decoration when they see it, eh, Cricket?"

Captain Kingsley's gaze swung back to her.

"Yes." Cricket shrugged and rolled out one of the maps again that showed an elaborate compass rose. "Sometimes, we get carried away."

"And the other four maps?" Now, Captain Kingsley's voice was like a shark, circling its prey.

He wouldn't give up easily. Penelope struggled to keep her gaze from going to the staircase to her room, where a dozen sea serpent maps lay hidden under her bed.

Santiago continued, "Three others were doubtful. Maybe the mapmaker or someone he talked to had actually seen a sea serpent. But not where they drew it."

He paused again and walked around a few bins. "But there was one map—" He picked up a couple rolls and looked at the bottom of the bin. "I wonder where it's gotten to?" He looked at Cricket, but she concentrated on rolling up the last map and refused to meet his eye.

Santiago paused. "I remember. I sold it just before Christmas."

"Who has it?" Captain Kingsley's eye didn't leave Santiago's face.

"The Captain of the *Cormorant*. Captain Eznick."

The fastest ship to leave harbor this spring, Penelope thought. Did he really sell a map to Captain Eznick?

Cricket spoke up. "Yes, I remember you told me about that sale. I was out the day he came in. You said he bought it on a lark."

Penelope nodded in relief: Cricket was supporting Santiago now. Whatever they were mad about would wait until the Captain was gone.

"Zee *Cormorant*," Frenchie said. "When did she leave dock? Where was she 'eading?"

"Not so fast," growled Captain Kingsley. "Tell me about the map."

Santiago described a crudely drawn map. To Penelope, it sounded too much like her original sea serpent map. Why was he describing that?

Santiago said, "It's in bad shape, that's for sure, and it's very old. But if you wanted to find a sea serpent, I'd look at that map first. Is that what you want? To find a sea serpent?"

Penelope's heart beat fast, waiting for the answer. Because if the answer was yes, then she wanted to sail on his boat. He'd be a hard Captain, but the chance of seeing a sea serpent might be worth it. She had heard so many sea serpent stories by now that she had started to doubt certain things. She wanted a first-hand look at these creatures.

Captain Kingsley took his time answering the question, so that Penelope almost leaned in close to pull the words from him. Why did he want that map?

At last, Captain Kingsley just laughed. "Sea serpents are just stories. I'm a collector. Of maps. That's all."

Frenchie sniggered behind his tiny wing. "A map collector."

"Wait, Frenchie." Captain Kingsley looked offended. "You make light of my collection." He spread out his huge paws to Cricket and the pigs, as if to seek their understanding. "Collecting is all consuming. It's a physical, mental and visual experience that moves me greatly. My collection of—" he turned to give Frenchie a stern look, "—of maps reminds me of the terrors of land and sea, the struggle for survival, the wildness that this world of Liberty almost crushed in us."

His voice was harsh. Penelope could imagine him hunting seals, an Arctic predator, a ruthless hunter. When she overheard the Captain and Frenchie on the *Hallowe'en*, had they been talking about a map collection? But why would they keep maps in icehouses around the world? They couldn't collect sea serpents because they didn't know where to find any. That's why they wanted the map. None of it made sense. But the Captain was obsessive about some kind of collection, and the map had something to do with it.

"I want my collection complete," Captain Kingsley whispered.

And the whisper—so full of longing—struck a chill into Penelope in a way that a shout or a loud demand could never have done.

Frenchie coughed.

The Captain shook himself and in an instant changed back from a predator to a gentleman and businessman. "I'm sorry. I go on too long."

The map shop suddenly seemed smaller as the Captain and his first mate rose.

"Thank you for your information," said Captain Kingsley, brisk and businesslike now. "We'll look for Captain Eznick." He left, followed by Frenchie.

Oddly, the shop was overtaken by a soundless void. Cricket collapsed into the chair by her desk.

But then the Captain filled the doorway again. "You, pig. Our navigator resigned today. Would you like the post of navigator on the *Hallowe'en*? I'll pay a bonus if you search every port we stop in for sea serpent maps. You'll know the real thing when you see it, won't you?"

Santiago drew in a sharp breath and darted a glance at Penelope. "Navigator?"

Going to sea with Captain Kingsley? She ran through the list of other captain and ships and realized Captain Kingsley might be exactly what they wanted. They'd certainly see the world since he meant to visit every icehouse he owned. And they might get to see a real sea serpent.

Impatient, Captain Kingsley said, "You know maps, right? You can read a sextant and keep us on course?"

"Yes, sir."

"Then, it's settled." Captain Kingsley turned and ducked under the doorframe, but rose too soon, scraping his shoulders on the frame.

"Wait."

The polar bear turned back impatiently. His massive paws hung on the top of the doorframe, letting his head hang low enough to see back inside. He glared—with his one good eye—at Santiago.

Penelope shivered as she remembered the sightless eye behind the patch.

"Penelope here," Santiago said. "She's my wife, and we've vowed to go to sea together."

Now the polar bear's gaze turned full upon her. Penelope let her mind go blank and returned his stare; this strategy had often worked on the docks when someone threatened to get too aggressive.

"What can you do besides load a ship and try to drown yourself?" Captain Kingsley asked.

"Sail. Climb riggings. Furl and unfurl. Haul anchor. Sing shanties. Load and unload. Cook."

"Cook?" Frenchie tilted his head until Penelope was afraid his beret would fall off. "Cook what?"

Remembering the scene at Fresh Pond, Penelope said, "Fish. Stew."

"Done. Navigator and assistant cook. Will it do?" Captain Kingsley asked.

"No," Penelope said, surprised at her own boldness. "I want to be a sailor, not a cook."

Captain Kingsley pulled out a pocket watch, studied it, and then returned it to its pocket. He swiveled his massive head, staring first at Santiago, then Penelope. His voice was a low rumble. "I've never had a hoofed animal as a sailor. Can you climb the riggings?"

"Yes, sir," Penelope answered without hesitation. "I've been practicing."

Captain Kingsley's head bobbed, "Sailor, then. You can try. Navigator and sailor. Will it do?"

Penelope wished she had time for a long talk with Santiago. Captain Kingsley would be a hard captain. She shrugged at Santiago and held her breath.

"Yes or no?" Captain Kingsley insisted.

A huge grin spread across Santiago's dark face. "Yes!"

To them both, Captain Kingsley said, "We sail at high tide. Tonight. Be on board the *Hallowe'en* by six." He was already out the door. "Frenchie, find out what you can about the *Cormorant*."

They disappeared down the street.

Cricket's voice was full of tears. "Tonight at high tide. On the *Hallowe'en*."

"Sooner than we thought," Penelope whispered.

"We're going to sea!" whooped Santiago, and drew them both into an ecstatic dance.

10

GOOD-BYES

If the Talberts were going to sea that very evening, there was no time to waste. Penelope sent Santiago out to buy new clothes, duffel bags, and a stock of parchment and journals.

As soon as he bustled out the door, Cricket said, "Upstairs."

Penelope agreed. They had to decide what to do with the two-dozen sea serpent maps she had bought all year. Santiago hadn't seen all the maps that had come into the store.

Penelope closed the stairway door and the shutters. Turning from the window, her heart was full. She and Santiago had made the tiny room into a home: Three of his hand-drawn maps were tacked to the wall, while the fourth wall was decorated with knotted ropes Penelope had made while practicing tying, not an easy task for her hoofed feet. The first few were uneven, but, by using her teeth as a third hand, she had improved. A tiny cotton quilt—imported from India—covered the bed. It would go, she decided, stuffing it into her duffle. Things were about to change drastically, and she wanted something familiar.

Cricket knelt and pulled maps from under the bed. "Will you take these with you?"

"No!" Penelope surprised herself at the force of her answer. She took a deep breath. "Why does Captain Kingsley want to find sea serpents? That's the question. What will he do when he finds them? I don't know if we can trust him."

"I don't know either," Cricket said. "He's dangerous. Be very, very careful around him."

"Sea serpents," Penelope's voice turned dreamy. "Do you think they are real? I've heard so many stories about these creatures, and now –" Penelope sat heavily on the bed. "Are they serpents because we name them that? Are they good instead of evil? I don't know."

"You think they are intelligent creatures?" Cricket asked in surprise.

"Maybe. I've collected many stories about sea serpents rescuing boats from a storm." Penelope shrugged. "Maybe Captain Kingsley is only interested in the maps, like he said. Whatever the case, I won't be responsible for helping Captain Kingsley capture a sea serpent. We'll keep our own secrets about maps until we know more."

"I'll keep these maps safe," Cricket said. "When you come back, I'll have them."

Below, the shop bell rang sharply.

"Santiago's back!" Penelope said.

Before they could do anything, Santiago burst into the room. He stopped short. "Ah. Your sea serpent maps."

Penelope flushed. So, he'd known about them all along.

Then, Santiago stood taller: "I have something to confess. Your map, the old one–"

"Where is it?" Penelope shuffled through the maps, looking for the flat-folded one.

"I borrowed and copied it," Santiago said. At Penelope's glare, he held up a hoof. "Let me explain. Sea serpents maps sell well. You were buying all the real ones," he shrugged, "so I made three copies of the old map."

Penelope stamped in anger, and her hooves rang in the tiny room. "Where are they?"

"That's just it. They're sold. In each copy, I moved the island a few degrees one direction or another. It can't be used to find the island. Not really."

Penelope burst out. "You copied my map!"

"You wasted money on them. Boat money." Santiago's voice was tight with anger.

"You don't know the stories," Penelope whispered.

"And you hid the maps from me."

"The stories," Penelope's voice grew stronger with conviction. "Sea serpents are intelligent creatures."

"Then tell me a story about sea serpents."

"There's not time. We've got to go." What a mess she'd made of everything. Santiago was right; she shouldn't have bought the maps behind his back and hid them. But he didn't understand. He hadn't listened to the stories like she had. Sea serpents deserved a chance. She wouldn't be responsible for helping Captain Kingsley capture one. She shivered. Or kill one. Suddenly, she didn't want Captain Kingsley to ever find a sea serpent. In fact, she needed to make sure he never found one. "I'm sorry. But there's not time," she repeated unhappily.

Cricket thumped the stack of maps. "There's time to answer me this: Why did you sell sea serpent maps behind my back?"

Santiago flushed, and the white blaze on his forehead turned pink with shame. "Extra boat money. It seemed harmless."

"Harmless?" Cricket was indignant.

"I never said they were original maps," Santiago said.

"Harmless? You cheated the customers," Cricket said, her voice was hard with anger.

"I let them assume," Santiago said.

"You risked my reputation, not just yours." Cricket waved toward the shop downstairs. The storage bins held samples, but their stock of the most popular maps were stacked neatly in cubbyholes. Everything she had built up over the years depended on her reputation.

Santiago's big shoulders sagged. "I didn't mean to cause you problems."

Cricket snapped, "No. You just thought of yourself and your needs. Well, now, it's your problem in a big way. Captain Kingsley thinks there's only one original map out there. What if he finds all the copies, too? Who will he suspect?"

They all thought about that. Penelope finally said, "It's too dangerous to ship out with him." She wanted to get ahead in the world, and she wanted to sail, but she also wanted to live.

"Where else can we get positions as navigator and sailor?" Santiago asked.

"This is what we've been looking for," Penelope added. "We can always blame another mapmaker."

"Cheating again!" Cricket cried.

"You're right. I created this problem; I'll take care of it." Santiago paced the tiny room.

"It's too dangerous," Penelope repeated.

"It's a risk we have to take," Santiago insisted. "We've signed on. If we skip out now, Kingsley will have us in jail."

Penelope leaned her dark face on her hooves. "OK. So there are fake maps out there. If Captain Kingsley finds a map, it won't endanger the sea serpents because it's fake."

"Maybe."

"What?"

"Maybe. The oldest map—I sold it accidentally. I thought it was a copy and didn't unfold it to check. There are three copies and one original out there."

Penelope's groan filled the tiny room. "It's possible Captain Eznick actually has the real one."

Santiago nodded helplessly.

A thought brightened Penelope's face. "Perhaps it's a bad map anyway."

Cricket rose now and paced, pushing the pigs onto the tiny bunk in her fury. Her long braid swished gently against the back of her silk trousers. "I won the map in a poker game in Indonesia. An old sailor—he was really ancient—pulled it out and tried to use it as a bet. No one else would give him a copper coin for it, but I gave him ten gold pieces. And later, I bought him drinks while he told me about the sea serpents. It's real. There are serpents on that island." Nervously, she rolled three maps together. "I wish I had never seen that map."

Penelope glared at Santiago, "You shouldn't have meddled with my maps." And she wondered if her anger wasn't partly a cover for her fear.

Santiago said, "You shouldn't have hidden them from me." His retort was weak, though, and Penelope thought he was scared, too.

Cricket broke the impasse: "We don't have time to argue. Santiago, you'll have to think of something before you catch up to Captain Eznick. Penelope, get these rolled up, and I'll hide them for you."

They turned attention to the task of getting ready to sail that evening. Penelope stripped the rest of the Talberts belongings from the room and tied them into two neat bundles, which Santiago packed into the duffle bags he had brought.

As she worked, Penelope thought about the upcoming journey. She had two goals, and she worried that they were mutually exclusive. Captain Kingsley had saved her life. She didn't put him on a pedestal and worship him for his actions that day; they were natural and easy actions for a polar bear. But she still felt like she owed him something; she wanted to repay the debt. On the other hand, she worried about the Captain's passion for these sea serpent maps. Sea serpents had to be intelligent creatures; nothing else made sense from the stories she'd heard. And how did his mysterious collection fit in with all this? If the Captain meant harm to sea serpents in any way, she would oppose him. Somehow she had to balance the need to repay a debt with the desire to protect sea serpents, of all things. Life, Penelope thought wryly, was strange.

Before they left, Cricket held out a bag with 50 gold coins to Santiago. "In every port, Captain Kingsley will have you looking for sea serpent maps," she said. "Buy any likely looking map, sea serpent or not. You'll know what I want. I'll split the profit with you when we sell them." She shrugged. "Extra boat money, without the cheating."

Impulsively, Santiago hugged her. "I'll never cheat a customer again."

"I know." She dropped the moneybag into his arms.

And finally, Penelope and Santiago went out into the shining afternoon and made their way to the *Hallowe'en*.

* * *

That evening, Mr. Ferco, the harbormaster, completed his log of the day's activities in Boston Harbor: "The *Hallowe'en* departed at dusk, washing out with the tide. Captain Kingsley has taken the helm of the flagship of his ice fleet."

Mr. Ferco closed the log with a snap, stood, and put on his derby. He yawned and pulled on his handlebar mustache. He paused in his office doorway to watch the lantern-lighters progress around the south side of the water.

Suddenly a fresh smell, like a farmyard after a rain, swept over Mr. Ferco. Looking up, he saw the *Hallowe'en* reach the harbor's entrance, where her sails filled and she leapt toward the open sea.

And Penelope and Santiago were sailors at last.

11

PIGS AT SEA

All Penelope could think about was going aloft. From the time she met Santiago, she knew this moment would come. Her stomach was queasy, not from seasickness, but from anticipation. As the boat put out to sea, they tried to sleep. Instead, Penelope listened to the shanties which rang out as sail after sail was unfurled. Finally, she dozed fitfully.

At dawn on their first day out to sea, Penelope and Santiago reported for the early morning watch. Her stomach still hadn't settled down, so she didn't eat breakfast. The sky was clear, the breeze, fresh. She stopped at the rail and stared at the dark blue sea where the currents ran so deep. Why hadn't she learned to swim after the incident at Fresh Pond? It had been too cold until just recently, and when the weather warmed, the stevedore business had picked up, leaving her no time.

The mate called, "First watch, over here."

Santiago was sent to the poop deck, the deck open to the weather at the stern, or rear, of the boat, to consult with the steersman. Penelope lined up with the other sailors. Frenchie's long beak jabbed here and there as he gave quiet but forceful orders to the crew. Finally, only Penelope was left.

"Swab the deck." Frenchie's beak jabbed at the bucket and brush beside the main mast.

Of course, she thought with a sigh. *I'll start at the bottom.*

She took the bucket, dropped it into the ocean and pulled up a full load. Swish! Water ran over the deck. She pushed the brush around with her hooves.

While she worked, Frenchie took turns sending sailors up the rigging, trying out each sailor's skills to see where they would best suit the working of the ship. The sails, from the bottom up, were the main-sail, lower-main-top-sail, upper-main-top-sail, main-gallant, main-royal and main-sky-sail. These sails were repeated on the foremast, toward the front, and the mizzenmast, toward the back. Some sailors did better at the higher altitudes of the sky-sails than others, who were better at handling the heavier sails toward the bottom.

Penelope concentrated on the smooth boards of the deck, trying to keep her anxiety under control. Would he never call her? Would she be allowed aloft today?

Penelope was an awkward climber, and she knew it; she had tried many methods, but without hands and fingers, she had few choices of climbing techniques. She had done chin ups and lifted weights, so she was confident her upper body strength was good enough to haul herself upward by wrapping a line around her foreleg and hooking it into the cleft of her hoof.

Still, she worried. She could brag about her abilities to furl and unfurl, but in reality, her skills aloft were untested.

She pulled up another boring bucket of water and looked longingly at the ropes above her.

"Odd, Beefie, Penelope. Tighten the mainsail." Frenchie's shiny beak jabbed upward.

Finally. She was going to do the work of a sailor. She was going to be a sailor.

She dumped out the bucket over the rail and eagerly started climbing the rigging along with the other two sailors, the only experienced sailors on their watch. Above her, moaning in the breeze, were acres of canvas.

She was glad her first orders were to take care of the mainsail, and she didn't have to climb far. She climbed with determination—awkward, but making steady progress. But when she was only halfway up, the others had already reached the top of the mainsail. They balanced on the yard, the horizontal wooden crosspiece, and sang a shanty while they pulled on lines. Odd—an odd name for a sailor—was the shanty man; he was skinny, with frizzy, wind-blown hair. It was a shanty Penelope recognized, and she joined in, singing happily as she climbed.

Aloft, it was windier, with a brisk breeze that cooled her brow. By the time she reached the mainsail's yard, though, the job was done, and the other sailors were descending.

Her heart dropped. After two years of dreaming of this moment, she was slow and clumsy. She stood on the mast's yardarm; her hooves couldn't grip the wood like men's toes or a polar bear's paws. Carefully, she balanced and wrapped a line around one foreleg.

The sky, the water, the wind—she soaked in the glorious moment. It smelled wet and salty and sweet. Around her, the sails were alive and crooning. Joy filled her like the wind filled the sails: this is what it was like to be a sailor.

A sudden gust caught her, and her hooves slipped on the smooth wood, plunging her downward. She dangled by her foreleg. Desperately, she swung her hind legs toward the yard, but she was hanging too far away. Then the wind twisted the ropes. No! It wasn't fair! Then, just like that–she was falling.

As she fell, she heard a cry: "Man overboard!"

Penelope fell and fell. She plunged past the warm upper layer into cold water. Panicked, she kicked hard. Kick, kick. Kick, kick. And finally, she bobbed to the surface. She gulped air. The surface was warm and glittery with sunlight. The dunking actually made her queasy stomach feel better. But she couldn't swim. She went down again.

Angrily, she kicked all four legs. It was awkward and tiring, but she found she could keep her head above water. Barely. She didn't make forward progress, but she didn't sink, either.

The ship had raced forward, but she could see it was starting to turn and come around to pick her up. Despair flooded through her. She had only been on the mainsail, and it was a clear day with a gentle breeze.

When she stood dripping before Captain Kingsley, the polar bear drummed his hairy paws on the rails. "Foolish pig! What would you do if I send you aloft on a stormy day?"

She didn't have an answer. "I stood on the yardarm. The sails were singing for me."

"No." Captain Kingsley towered over her. "I should've known better. Hoofed creatures, intelligent or not, are a danger to our ship when they go aloft. You're grounded."

A great sadness filled her chest. She wanted to be competent aloft; she had tried to be. It was hard to keep the longing from her voice, "From the yardarm, the horizon looked so wide."

"No. You're the cook's assistant."

In the tight circle of sailors surrounding them, Penelope saw Santiago's dark face grimace. Her lack of skills reflected on him, too. Of course, he understood her disappointment, but he had the perfect job: navigators seldom had to climb the rigging. It wasn't fair!

Penelope shook herself, and then wiped her nose on her foreleg. Captain Kingsley was right. Her hooves handicapped her, and she was dangerous to herself and the ship.

An hour ago, she had still been blinded by her dreams; she would be an agile sailor, climbing through the rigging as nimbly as a monkey. Instead, she was betrayed by her body. She had a sailor's heart trapped in a pig's thick, clumsy torso; she was mocked by hooves instead of fingers. Bodies give creatures and humans certain possibilities and deny them others. A 300-pound gorilla couldn't dance ballet. A heron couldn't lift a 300-pound block of ice. But Penelope had never thought about her body this way. It hit her now with a heaviness in her muscles; on small sailboats, she and Santiago might manage, but not on larger ships where they had to climb rigging.

But an assistant cook? It was almost more than she could bear. It was hard to give up a dream. She was a crewmember of a tall ship, one of the fastest ships ever made. And on the first day, she was demoted to assistant cook.

Something else struck her, too. Captain Kingsley had known all along what would happen. He had known pigs couldn't climb. He didn't care if she was a sailor or an assistant cook, so long as he got Santiago to search for maps. This, she decided bitterly, was enough repayment for Captain Kingsley; to her, it would balance the scales of justice. She would serve willingly as assistant cook until they returned to Boston, but she owed him nothing else for saving her life. The only thing she would worry about now was the sea serpent question.

In her cabin, Penelope pulled a dry set of clothes from her footlocker.

Santiago came into the cabin, his face dark and worried. "When you fell overboard, I wanted to jump in after you. Frenchie wouldn't let me."

Shaking her head, Penelope tried to button her clothes. Cricket had replaced many of the hard-to-use buttons with Chinese frog closures; even these were particularly hard today. "You can't swim either. That would've been foolish."

"I know. But I wanted to do something. Captain Kingsley was harsh."

"No, he's right. I should never go aloft again."

Santiago's shoulders sagged. "This isn't how I wanted it to be."

Penelope shrugged. "There's nothing you can do." She pushed past him and reported to the cook. She knew she was being short with Santiago, but she needed time to adjust to this change.

Cactus, the cook, was the same small but stalwart porcupine who had served stew for the iceman at Fresh Pond, the one who had wrapped hot water bottles around her as she lay in the sleigh after nearly drowning.

"Tough luck," he said cheerfully. "But you're still at sea. And we've got lots of work to do. Do you know anything about cooking?"

"I've helped the cook at the Tea Party Inn."

Cactus tried to make her feel comfortable in the tiny galley, but it was laid out for his compact body and agile hands. Counters were low, and drawers were awkwardly spaced for her. He set her to work peeling potatoes, but she was clumsy with the knife. He set her to stirring the huge pot of stew, instead. Finally, he set her to washing dishes, which was easy since the plates were tin and unbreakable.

That night, after their first full day of sailing, Penelope and Santiago were so tired they threw themselves into the small bunk they shared in the navigator's quarters. At least Penelope didn't have to stay in the damp forecastle with the other crewmen. But it was little comfort. She lay awake remembering how glorious it felt to stand at the top of the mainsail with the wind in her face.

For Penelope, the moment had been too brief.

12

WIND

Life at sea was hard; nature made sure of that. Life on the *Hallowe'en* was even harder because the crew had to please Captain Kingsley, and he allowed for no weaknesses in his crew. "Eight days from now, we'll catch the *Cormorant* in St. George's Harbor in Bermuda," he declared. "I want that map."

Everything was focused on speed, which meant the ship had to run at top efficiency.

Meanwhile, Santiago was having his own difficulties. He was on his feet all day, running errands for Frenchie or the other officers, or fetching and putting up maps. He had to pay attention to the sky and the sea and the sails and the wind and anticipate how all these affected their course. The past year, spent hunched over a desk, had ill prepared him for the tasks he was now required to perform with speed, efficiency, and courtesy.

Fortunately, Captain Kingsley was a good navigator himself. His white hulk often towered over Santiago as he checked Santiago's figures. In snatches of conversation between tasks, Santiago told Penelope that the Captain might look like all muscle and sound like a dictator, but he had a sharp intelligence and a knack for calculating in his head.

After two days of sailing, though, Santiago complained to Penelope while they readied for bed. "We are using outdated maps." He tapped one of his own maps, which was spread out on their bunk. "Look: we're here. But according to Lt. Maury's charts, we'd have better wind to the west."

Penelope studied the map. "If we keep this course, we risk being stuck with no wind for days. Captain Kingsley wants to be there in six days. Show him your map."

Santiago nodded. "You're right. These are important maps, not because I made them, but because I'm right. Besides," he said in a half joking manner, "I'm a master mapmaker; my maps deserve respect."

His pride was showing again, Penelope thought. But if pride gave him foolish attitudes, it was also the source of his ambition, and they needed that ambition to get ahead in this world. Since Penelope was already demoted, Santiago needed to shine all the more.

Penelope thumped his back. "He hired you out of Cricket's map shop. He knows that you understand maps. Be brave."

She fought the bitterness about her own failures that tried to overwhelm her. Instead, she put all her feelings behind her and vowed to help Santiago succeed, for them both.

The next morning, Santiago knocked at Captain Kingsley's cabin door. Penelope stood behind him to bolster his courage. They had dressed in their best uniforms and polished their hooves.

Captain Kingsley's voice boomed, "Who is it?"

"Excuse me, sir. It's Santiago Talbert. I'd like to show you something."

There was a short pause and the sound like a door shutting. And then, "Come in."

For a captain's cabin, the room was tiny; a wide bunk took up the port side, a birdcage with a green parrot took up half the floor. The cage door was missing, so the parrot could fly around as it wanted. No intelligent creature liked caging up another animal. The parrot was seldom seen outside the captain's cabin, but they often heard him talking, "Captain, Captain, Captain."

The birdcage only left space for a tiny desk and chair. Confused at the small size of the cabin, Penelope looked closer. In the ebony paneling behind the desk was a door. It looked like the captain's quarters had been divided for some reason into this tiny room and another room, the purpose of which she could only guess. Captain Kingsley seldom let any crewman except Frenchie into his room, so there wasn't any ship gossip about it.

Looking up, Captain Kingsley motioned for Santiago and Penelope to stand at ease.

Santiago held up a parchment. "May I?"

Captain Kingsley nodded toward the desk.

Penelope gingerly closed the logbook and put it on the bunk, so Santiago could spread the chart on the desk.

"These are the latest charts from Lt. Maury," Santiago said.

"Those." Captain Kingsley rolled his eyes, and then bent to gaze out the porthole.

Santiago pointed toward the Atlantic, where currents and winds were charted. "These should help us go faster."

Captain Kingsley stood with his legs wide apart, his paws clasped behind his back. He didn't turn to look at Santiago or the map. "Lt. Maury is a landlubber."

"He's studied ships' logs. Thousands."

Penelope was surprised at Captain Kingsley's scorn. Boston had been full of praise for Lt. Maury's work. But she'd also heard that some Captains refused to look at the charts because Lt. Maury had never commanded a ship.

"Studied," Captain Kingsley said in scorn.

Santiago tried again. "Without the charts, it's like sailing blind."

Captain Kingsley's voice took on a deadly calm. "I know these seas."

"Of course, sir."

"That's it, then. Dismissed."

Reluctantly, Santiago rolled up his charts, jammed them under his arm and saluted.

Back in their cabin, Santiago threw the maps onto the bunk. "Why wouldn't he look?"

Penelope stored the charts under their bunk. "Change is hard. They're good charts, and we'll need them some day. Maybe soon. Captain Kingsley wants to reach Bermuda in five days, and he won't make it on the present course. Be patient."

Fortunately, their life was too busy to worry much about maps. Because of their different positions on the ship, Penelope and Santiago learned to get along with different groups. As navigator, Santiago was expected to eat with the officers; as cook's assistant, Penelope ate and worked with the crew.

"They're standoffish," Penelope complained.

"They don't quite trust my navigation," Santiago complained.

That night, Odd, the shanty man, banged on the door of the navigator's cabin and insisted Penelope and Santiago come on deck to see something astonishing.

It was so dark that only pure white was visible: the white blaze on Santiago's face, Penelope's white forelegs, and Odd's white shock of hair.

Odd handed a telescope to Santiago. "Look to the east. You'll see a green glow in the water. Phosphorescent algae."

Santiago held the telescope to his eye. Nothing but black sky, black water and brilliant stars.

"Let me try," Penelope said.

"Yes," Odd said. "Let her try."

Penelope hesitated at the laughter in Odd's voice. But she looked through the telescope; she saw nothing unusual, either. Aggravated at the loss of sleep, they tumbled back into their bunks and snored until the ship's bell turned them out an hour before dawn. Still dark, they stumbled to their stations.

When Cactus saw her, he stopped abruptly and started laughing. Behind him, Frenchie sniggered behind his tiny wing.

"What's wrong?" Penelope said.

Cactus laughed all the harder and refused to answer.

Penelope checked her clothes, but everything was right side out and buttoned correctly. She stood straighter, but when the third mate saw her, he laughed, too. What was going on?

Penelope disliked the long hours in the galley without ever seeing the sky. That made one of her favorite duties carrying coffee to those on duty; it was a chance to be outside. This morning, she climbed the steps to the poop deck. She handed steaming mugs to the officers there. When she saw Santiago, they both stopped short.

"You've got a—"

"You've got a—"

They both had a white ring of paint around their eyes; Odd had dipped the telescope into paint before they looked through it. And the whole crew was in on the joke.

"—a bull's eye," finished Penelope.

"And it's the funniest thing I've ever seen," Santiago added.

His great belly laugh filled the ship until everyone, crew and officers, was laughing, too.

Because the Talberts took the prank in stride, they were more readily accepted by both crew and mates. They had passed an initiation of sorts.

On the fifth day out, they hit the doldrums. The wind slackened, and the sails hung limp. Santiago paced their tiny room and complained, "According to Lt. Maury's maps, if we were fifty miles west, we'd have winds. Not stiff winds, but enough to keep us moving."

Penelope said, "Talk to the Captain. He wants to be in Bermuda in three days."

Instead Santiago fumed all that day.

At dawn the next day, he clutched his maps and stomped out of their room, mumbling to himself. "Two days. Only two days."

Penelope followed him to the deck above. The boat was quiet; no water was shushing past their ship, no wind moaning, and no singing by the shanty man. They were dead in the water.

Using his sextant, Santiago took his sighting of the morning stars and charted the *Hallowe'en*'s position. When his watch began at eight bells, he ordered the wheel turned to head farther west.

Penelope had to admire Santiago. He was foolhardy, yes, but he was also brave. He did what he knew was right, even when he knew the Captain would be mad. It was a bold move, and Penelope was proud of him.

And now they had to wait. Either Frenchie or Captain Kingsley would stand the next watch in four hours. When they came on duty, they would check their position. Santiago had four hours to find wind.

The first hour passed slowly, with no changes; they were still dead in the water.

The second hour, the sails still hung limp, but it seemed a lazy current tugged at them. They moved sluggishly.

Santiago stopped by the kitchen to whisper to Penelope. "If we had more time. This current should pull us toward a corridor of wind. It's on my charts."

But they only had two hours left.

Now there was a whisper of wind, just enough to taunt the sails and remind them of their function. But not enough to move the tall ship. Then, just as suddenly as it began, the slight wind died, and the current slowed.

The ship's hourglass turned again. Half an hour till the end of their watch. A quarter hour. The sun was hot; the water, glaring. Sailors dipped rags in the water and wrapped them around their necks to cool off.

Just a whisper of wind returned. Finally a puff of wind filled the sails, making them flap before leaving them limp again. Penelope felt the change and leaned out the galley's door. Where was the wind? They had to find it.

The hourglass was almost spent. Santiago called to the helmsman, "Head due southwest, please."

The helmsman spun the great wheel, until the *Hallowe'en* was aligned with the compass, heading straight southwest. Slowly, steadily, the sails filled with wind, as if it was being poured straight out of a bottle into the canvas itself.

Precisely at noon, when the ship's bell rang and the hourglass was turned, Captain Kingsley emerged from his cabin and climbed the ladder to the poop deck. He stopped halfway up the stairs and squinted upward. "Tighten that mainsail," he roared.

Santiago stopped in the galley's doorway to grin at Penelope. She looked up from the stew pot and grinned back.

"Good to hear him shouting orders again, isn't it?" she said. "He's pleased."

Off duty, Santiago waited until Penelope finished serving and was free to eat lunch. They leaned against the foremast, where they could feel the breeze that now blew.

From the poop deck, Penelope heard Frenchie roar. "Captain. We're fifty miles west of where we should be."

Captain Kingsley found Santiago a minute later. He began without a preamble. "Explain our position, Mister."

"Ah. Yes, sir." Santiago brushed breadcrumbs from his uniform and stood. "If I may?" He motioned to the charts beside him.

Penelope watched them climb the poop deck, where Santiago spread out the charts. There was lots of gesturing, and then the Captain slapped Santiago on the back, almost knocking him down.

"I let pride get the better of me," Captain Kingsley said. "You were right about Lt. Maury's charts."

Had Penelope heard right? Captain Kingsley had admitted he was wrong? She'd never heard a sea captain risk losing face like that. It made her warm to him, despite everything. *Santiago could take humility lessons from the Captain*, she thought with wonder.

Santiago's belly laugh rang out across the ship. He and the Captain looked up to where the mainsail was just starting to strain against the rigging.

"Unfurl the lower-main-topsail!" the Captain bellowed.

Santiago had taken a risk, and it had paid off. Penelope didn't like to think what would have happened if they hadn't found the wind. She didn't think Captain Kingsley was a forgiving sort.

Still, the doldrums had set them behind. After nine days at sea, they finally arrived at St. George's, one of the most beautiful tropical islands in Bermuda. They learned the *Cormorant* had left just two days before, with a load of oranges to deliver to St. Michaels in Maryland.

Captain Kingsley slammed his great paw on the center mast, making it shiver all the way up to the main-sky-sail. He vowed, "We'll catch the *Cormorant*, and I'll have that map before the end of the week. Or else."

They only stayed in harbor long enough to take on fresh water, no fresh food.

And the chase was on.

Tension ran high amongst the crew. Each order from an officer was carried out with exacting speed, aided by Odd's fast-paced shanties. Everyone's eye constantly went to Hammer, the crewman with the sharpest eyes, who was posted in the crow's nest with a telescope.

Because there wasn't a quarry visible on the horizon, the hourly calculation of their speed was their only measure of how close they were to their goal. Under Frenchie's supervision, they dropped a rope into the wake, counting how many fathoms it paid out in thirty seconds, and then calculated their speed; each time, it was higher.

But Captain Kingsley wasn't satisfied. Each time, he bellowed, "More sail!"

This sent the crewmen aloft, unfurling more and more canvas, until they ran under full sail. The *Hallowe'en* flew across the waves, as graceful as a black swan.

At last, at dawn on the third day, Hammer called from the crow's nest, "Sails on the horizon!"

And so, the *Hallowe'en* found the *Cormorant* while they were both still at sea. Between signal flags and small boats carrying messages back and forth, it was finally decided that Captain Kingsley would host Captain Eznick on the *Hallowe'en* at dusk for dinner. And the orangutan would bring with him a certain map.

13

THE CAPTAINS' STORIES

In preparation for the meeting of the Captains, the crew scrubbed the deck until it shone. Frenchie dove into the water and fished, catching three sea bass for their meal; everyone else helped Cactus peel vegetables or set up tables on deck for the meal.

All afternoon, as she scurried about the galley, Penelope felt the pressure building. Santiago should easily be able to tell if the sea serpent map was real or one of his copies. That left two questions: If it was the real map, did they want the Captain to have it? And why was the Captain searching for sea serpents?

The Atlantic cooperated that evening with fair weather. For this meal, the tin plates were replaced with the Captain's best china and silverware. Cactus insisted that small railings be used on the table's edge to prevent the expensive table settings from falling off, in case of an unexpected swell or wave. But it wasn't necessary, so calm was the sea.

Just at dusk, the rowboat from the *Cormorant* arrived.

Captain Eznick, the orangutan, was resplendent in his blue uniform and shiny brass buttons, while Captain Kingsley wore a black uniform with gold buttons, with a black satin eye-patch. Neither wore shoes, but both had curved swords strapped onto their waists.

Everything was black and white on the *Hallowe'en*: bone-white china, white tablecloth, black chairs. The mates' uniforms were black, while the rest of the crew wore dress-white, and even Frenchie, who normally didn't wear clothes, put on a black bow-tie and black beret and looked like he was in a formal tuxedo. Black and white. Penelope almost expected to look overhead and see a flag with the wicked skull-and-crossbones. She shivered. What would happen tonight?

The Captains' conversation during the meal was about shipping gossip: who was hauling what to where? Penelope chafed at the chitchat. Fortunately, she was assigned to serve Frenchie, which kept her mind off the real business of the evening. Likewise, each officer from both ships had a crewman to serve them.

Not until coffee was served did the topic turn to sea serpents. Though Penelope still stood at attention, she hung on every word.

Captain Eznick cupped the coffee mug in his hairy hands. "You look for a special map?"

"Yes. I believe Cricket Mansfield's shop sold you a map while you were there this winter," Captain Kingsley said.

"It's old. Not any good for navigation."

"Then why did you buy it?"

Captain Eznick leaned forward. "Each of us has a story about moving from our small worlds into Liberty where intelligent creatures can make their way. Mine is a story of dumb luck."

Startled, Penelope realized he was going to tell about his crossing. Few spoke of their own crossing, almost as if their old life had never existed. Were they ashamed that the other world existed? She didn't know, but she and Santiago had seldom told their story, either.

"My mother was captured when I was just a small thing." Captain Eznick made a cradling motion with his arms. "From what my father said, they carried her off to the London Zoo, where, for all I know, she still lives."

At the word "zoo," Frenchie sat up straighter and turned to stare at the orangutan.

Penelope, watching from behind Frenchie's chair, was surprised. Nothing seemed to phase Frenchie; why the word, "zoo"?

"For my part," Captain Eznick continued, "I left the jungle and took passage on a sail boat crossing from Africa to Barbados; it was my crossing into Liberty. In the middle of the Atlantic, a hurricane slammed into our boat. It tossed us and turned us, but somehow we managed to stay afloat for a day, then two days. We hoped the hurricane would blow over soon, and we'd be safe. But sometime in that second night, the storm grew worse, until at the gray dawn, we saw we were breaking up. We feared all hands would be lost.

"Then the most amazing thing happened. We were cold from the storm. We were exhausted from two days of fighting the weather. But none of that mattered. Not when we saw rising above us the coils of a sea serpent.

"The sea serpent swam alongside us, towering overhead, even higher than the curl of the waves. It bumped our ship, and we thought we were gone. Then we stopped, without knowing why. By evening, the seas calmed, and we saw that we were beached on a strange island, one I'd never seen before or since on a map.

"I think the sea serpent pushed us onto that island. I think it saved our lives. Because of a sea serpent, I lived to find my way to Liberty."

Penelope sighed in satisfaction. It was what she heard over and over again from sailors: tales of rescue. She had yet to record a story where a sea serpent tried to eat anything—except in someone's imagination.

"It's the coils you remember," Captain Eznick said. "Like a snake, it coils around and around. When I saw the map with sea serpent coils, I had to have it."

"Frenchie and I have made our fortunes with maps," Captain Kingsley said. The good food and good wine had put him in a good humor and made him talkative. "We were crewmen on the *Tongass*, when we came across a map store in Anchorage, Alaska. The oldest map they had—and the cheapest, which is why we bought it—was a tattered treasure map. Gold doubloons were supposed to be buried in a cove on the Patagonia coast. We pooled our money and bought a tiny boat. Sailing around the Cape of Good Horn and up the South American coast to Patagonia took us a year. We had to stop at different ports and work for a while in order to buy supplies. Fortunately, Frenchie can catch a fish in any waters, or we would have starved."

Every *Hallowe'en* crewman was staring at Captain Kingsley. No one had heard this much of the Captain's story, not ever.

But Captain Kingsley wasn't finished. He tossed down another glass of wine and called to Cactus to bring another.

He continued with his story. "We found the right cove and dug. What do you think?" He leaned toward Captain Eznick and waited. At the orangutan's shrug, he rapped his knuckles on the table. "We found the treasure." He leaned back in his chair and whistled low. "Beautiful gold. It made us rich, eh, Frenchie?"

The penguin's voice was cold. "You tell too much. Be careful."

"We used that gold to start the ice trade. Oh, everyone thought it was a crazy idea, but we know about ice and snow and cold, don't we, Frenchie? A polar bear and a penguin. We're good businessmen." Captain Kingsley rose, a bit unsteady, and leaned onto the table. His voice became hard. "And I want that map."

Captain Eznick roared with laughter. "So dramatic! You won't want it."

"Why not?"

"It's a fake," Captain Eznick said. "Before we left Boston Harbor, I dined with Captains Brice, Nichols and Oakley."

Frenchie muttered, "Zee *Endurance*, zee *Loch Doon*, and zee *Elizabeth*."

"We all had a copy of the map. Each different. And each bought at a different map shop. Oh, each one was an accurate picture of North and South America, and the Caribbean. But each showed the sea serpent island in a different place. We passed them round and round, and in the end, I don't know if I have the same map I paid for. I doubt it makes much difference."

"Forgeries!" Captain Kingsley raised a fist to the moon where it sat full and yellow on the horizon. Then, his gaze fell on Santiago where he sat at the foot of the table. "Ah." His mood changed. He sat, and then turned courteously to Captain Eznick. "Then, I'd be glad to take that worthless map off your hands. Let my navigator examine it first."

Penelope was surprised that Captain Kingsley trusted Santiago's judgment so much. It made things even trickier. Santiago needed to tell the truth about the map if he could at all.

"I've already told you it's a forgery," Captain Eznick said. "Pay me first."

Captain Kingsley sighed. "What? A gold coin?"

"I paid ten gold coins for it."

Captain Kingsley's dark eye glittered dangerously, but his voice was calm: "Ten, it is."

"Done." Captain Eznick snapped his fingers. His first mate, a tall man with a bulging Adam's apple, rose and brought him a small packet.

Immediately, Frenchie was beside Captain Eznick, holding out a pouch of coins. He dropped it into the orangutan's hand and took the map. He marched around to Santiago, swept his dishes out of the way, and put the map on the table in front of him.

With every eye on him, Santiago tugged at the string around the map. Carefully, he unfolded it and set tea cups on each corner to hold it open.

Penelope wasn't surprised to see that the lower left corner was torn; Santiago would have duplicated that in each one. But was the map real or fake?

Cactus chose that moment to appear with flaming *crepes l'orange* for dessert. Penelope had helped Cactus make the crepes, thin dessert pancakes. The oranges for the sauce were, of course, supplied by Captain Eznick. The flaming dessert captured everyone's attention for the next few minutes, except for Santiago's. And Penelope's. She watched him closely, but he didn't look up. Was it a forgery? Reluctantly, she turned her attention to serving the crepes to Frenchie.

When everyone was served, the attention returned to Santiago. Over the chatter and sounds of eating, Captain Kingsley fixed Santiago with a fierce stare. By now, the lanterns had been lit, and the Captain's one good eye glittered darkly in his face. Captain Kingsley said, "Well? What do you think?"

Santiago shook his head. "Forgery, sir."

Penelope let out a sigh.

Captain Kingsley slammed his paw on the table, startling everyone. "Frenchie!"

"Yes, Captain. I understand." He turned to Captain Eznick. "What do you know of zee *Endurance*, zee *Loch Doon*, and zee *Elizabeth*?"

"The *Loch Doon* is headed for Bombay, and the *Elizabeth*, for Sydney. The *Endurance* is slow, so she only runs from Barbados to Boston. She should be back in Boston by now," Captain Eznick said. He hesitated. "I'd go after the *Elizabeth* first, and then the *Loch Doon*. The *Endurance* you can find easily whenever you want, but the other two travel the globe. I assume you want to find all four maps?"

And Penelope worried even more. When they finally found all four maps, including the original, what would Captain Kingsley do with them? Why did he want sea serpents so badly? They were no closer to the answer; all this had done was tease Captain Kingsley and make him want the other maps even more.

The lantern in the crow's nest made the mast and riggings cast dark shadows. This sailboat would be Penelope's and Santiago's world until they had all four sea serpent maps. How long would they live on the *Hallowe'en* before returning to Boston?

14

FRENCHIE'S CHEST

MAY. HEADING SOUTH.

They chased the *Elizabeth* and Captain Oakley south, towards Sydney, Australia. Penelope loved the warm tropics and was thrilled when they crossed the equator. But as the Southern Cross constellation came into view, she found she and Santiago had switched places. Now that Santiago had a stable position in the crew, he became complacent, content to put in his watch, then sleep. But Penelope rarely slept. She wanted to be something besides the cook's assistant. Ambition. She had more of it than Santiago now. But it didn't feel like ambition to her; it felt like frustration. What other task could she perform on this ship? The question sent her prowling the ship, watching, watching, watching.

Unexpectedly one evening they put into the port at Rio de Janeiro. Darkness veiled the city; only the mountain, which towered over the harbor, was visible. No one was allowed shore leave except Frenchie. He left with a small, carved chest that he pushed along in a wheelbarrow. He returned six hours later just as the watch changed at midnight. The crew getting off duty was already below. The crew coming on duty was crowded near the galley, getting cups of coffee. Only Penelope—watching everything—saw Frenchie return. Silently, he lugged the chest aboard and laid it at the Captain's feet.

"From zee icehouse," Frenchie said softly.

In the starlight, the Captain's white face smiled, showing his yellow teeth. He heaved the chest onto his shoulder and carried it to his cabin. When it was safely stowed, he gave the orders to leave port.

Obviously, Frenchie had brought the Captain part of their collection from the Rio de Janeiro icehouse. Whatever they collected, it wasn't large, or it wouldn't fit in such a small chest. What, Penelope wondered, were they collecting?

JULY. ROUNDING CAPE HORN, SOUTHERN TIP OF SOUTH AMERICA.

July in the southern hemisphere is winter, and rounding Cape Horn challenged them all. On Santiago's maps, Chile tapered to a point at Cape Horn, making him think it would be a quick passage; instead, it was long and full of fog and icebergs, waves and rocks, making it more difficult; the winter days held a few scant hours of daylight before sending them into darkness again. Unceasing, fierce winds tried to blow the *Hallowe'en* onto the rocks. They had to tack, back and forth, in heavy seas, hampered by cold, stiff hands or paws and weary bodies. The "All hands on deck" call came so frequently that no crewman had more than an hour's sleep at a time.

Only Captain Kingsley and Frenchie were comfortable: they discarded their sodden, cotton clothing and let their natural fur and feathers shed the water and cold. Polar bears have small bumps and cavities on the soles of their feet that act like suction cups, preventing the bears from slipping on the ice. When no one else could stand, Captain Kingsley spun the great wheel as if it were weightless. Frenchie swam through the foamy waves that pounded their decks.

Peeking out from the warm galley, Penelope thought of the first day she had seen Captain Kingsley, dining in style at the edge of Fresh Pond, regal and imposing: the Ice King. A superb businessman and a trendsetter in polite society. He was refined.

Here, in the Straits, that Captain Kingsley would not be recognized. With windblown fur, he moved with a loose-limbed grace, swinging his arms as if conducting the harsh symphony of frigid wind and water. He was a wild Ice King, bursting with a fierce joy.

SEPTEMBER. SYDNEY, AUSTRALIA.

Compared to the trip around the Horn, the run to Sydney was easy, and they arrived in early September. Frenchie found that the *Elizabeth* had just left port the week before, sailing for Hong Kong. Though Captain Kingsley wanted to follow immediately, they were forced to wait a week for the ice to be unloaded and provisions to be taken aboard. To help pay expenses, the Captain took on small shipments bound for Hong Kong, but no one had much interest in their new cargo. Penelope did notice, though, when Frenchie slipped off one day with the chest; when he returned later, it was very heavy, and Captain Kingsley quickly took it below.

Penelope and Santiago used the week to explore the thriving seaport. Tulips, imported from Holland, were blooming in the early spring weather of the southern hemisphere.

Penelope and Santiago located three map shops, where Santiago spent half of Cricket's gold coins. Penelope found two maps with sea serpents on them, but she resisted buying them because she didn't want to have them on Captain Kingsley's boat. Santiago saw them and bought them anyway.

"These serpents are just decoration," Santiago reassured Penelope. "It won't hurt to give them to Captain Kingsley."

"What will he do with sea serpents if he catches them?" Penelope asked.

The Talberts discussed this urgent question but came to no conclusion about Captain Kingsley's ultimate goals. But one thing was clear: they didn't trust him.

OCTOBER. BOMBAY, INDIA.

From Sydney to Hong Kong and Hong Kong to Bombay, they chased the *Elizabeth*. They loaded and unloaded minor cargoes at every port, but Captain Kingsley made sure that didn't slow him down. The Captain insisted on full sails as they crossed first the Pacific and then the Indian Ocean. By now, he always used Santiago's charts, which let them stay in currents where they could run under full sail.

Finally, in Bombay, they caught Captain Oakley. He was a British fox, with a long red tail. He refused to see Captain Kingsley; he was too busy, he said, until his ship was loaded. So Captain Kingsley fumed and waited.

Penelope and Santiago were anxious to see the town of Bombay, but Captain Kingsley allowed no shore leave, fearing the *Elizabeth* would try to slip out of harbor during the night. The *Elizabeth* was a small, swift barque, originally built for the tea trade to and from China, but now it carried cargo wherever she found it. She was loading cotton and would soon leave, bound for Boston Harbor.

Finally, tired of the waiting, Captain Kingsley took matters into his own hands and stomped over to the *Elizabeth* and roared for permission to board. Captain Oakley rushed onto deck.

"What is it you want?" Captain Oakley said. He stood on the poop deck, making sure he was higher than the tall polar bear.

"The sea serpent map you bought from a map shop in Boston."

Captain Oakley narrowed his eyes and flicked his tail suspiciously. "That's it?"

Captain Kingsley gave a curt nod.

"It cost me ten gold coins."

"I'll give you twenty."

"Done."

Santiago stared at the second map and compared it to the first. "Forgery," he told Captain Kingsley.

The Captain bellowed in frustration and paced back and forth, sending all the crewman below or aloft, out of his way. He didn't calm down until Frenchie returned an hour later.

The penguin stood on shore watching the Captain pacing for several minutes before he was noticed. When Captain

Kingsley finally saw him, Frenchie called out triumphantly, "I 'ave it." His wing caressed the mysterious carved chest.

Captain Kingsley brightened, and then disappeared, carrying the chest, into his cabin. For several hours, a strange sort of chemical smell came up from his cabin, but no noise.

Left to themselves, the crew took bets on what was in the chest: money, jewels, maps, spices, or holy relics. Penelope took all their money with her guess: a secret.

DECEMBER. CAPE TOWN, SOUTH AFRICA.

They sailed across the Indian Ocean bound for London, where Frenchie had heard the *Loch Doon* and Captain Nichols could be found. Captain Kingsley wanted that third sea serpent map.

They spent Christmas and New Year's Day in Cape Town, South Africa. Frenchie again slipped off to the icehouse and returned with a heavy chest. But an illness aboard ship kept the pigs from worrying about it this time.

Cactus caught a fever and couldn't cook, leaving the galley solely to Penelope. She went into town daily and explored the native fruits, vegetables and spices. The responsibility left her with no time to fret about wanting other jobs on the ship. She cooked, ate, cleaned up—and slept soundly for the first time in weeks. She was almost sad when Cactus returned to supervise the cooking again.

The fourth mate also fell ill in Cape Town, and though they waited a week for him to recuperate, he was still unable to sail. They left him there, making Santiago the fourth mate.

A month ago, Penelope would have been jealous of Santiago's promotion, but now she was enjoying her job in the galley. Contentment was a surprise to her after the ambition that had consumed her at the voyage's beginning. There was a pleasure in doing a job and doing it well, pleasure in the rhythms of the job: buying food, cooking, serving, cleaning up.

JANUARY. LISBON, PORTUGAL.

It was a leisurely sail up the African coast to Lisbon, Portugal where they put in for a month to resupply. Before the month in Lisbon ended, the mysterious chest reappeared again to Captain Kingsley's delight and the crew's frustrated speculation. Captain Kingsley fiercely guarded the privacy of his cabin, and no one dared even think of crossing him.

Penelope's guess about the contents of the chest stood: a secret.

When they sailed again, Penelope thought that going to sea was like going home. "I love sailing," Penelope told Santiago. "This is a good life."

FEBRUARY. LONDON, ENGLAND.

At London, when they finally arrived in late summer, they were stunned to learn Captain Nichols was dead: he had been washed overboard in a storm and drowned. His sea chest and all it contained had been sent to his widow in Dublin.

FEBRUARY. DUBLIN, IRELAND.

So, the *Hallowe'en* went to Dublin. But here, all trace of the widow had disappeared. Captain Kingsley hired detectives to find her, but it meant a long stay in port. The crew rotated standing watch, an easy duty because Captain Kingsley was gone most evenings visiting other sea captains. And unless they had watch, the crew had shore leave—though they were warned to stay close in case the *Hallowe'en* had to leave on short notice.

Penelope loved the Green Isle. She spent long hours in pubs listening to sea serpent stories, learning new sea shanties, and trying to speak with an Irish brogue. The first week there, she heard an old Irish woman playing a harp, and Penelope insisted on learning. She took harp lessons each morning; by the second week, she bought a small, carved Irish harp for herself. Though she couldn't pluck the strings, her hooves allowed her to strum them.

Meanwhile, Santiago haunted the map shops, hovering over the cartographers, and learning to draw Celtic knots to embellish his own maps. Sea serpent maps were everywhere in this land of superstition; it was as if the sea serpent was the national mascot.

Finally, the detective returned and reported that Widow Nichols had moved to her parent's home on the Isle of Man. Captain Kingsley ordered the *Hallowe'en* to be ready to sail within the hour. Every sailor was found except Odd the shanty man.

Captain Kingsley paced the deck for thirty minutes, scanning the shore, waiting for Odd to appear. Finally, he called Penelope to the poop deck.

"Can you still sing shanties?"

Penelope stared up at the polar bear and stammered. "Ye-yes, s-sir."

"Good. You're the new shanty man. My cabin boy will take your place as cook's assistant." He whirled and yelled to Frenchie. "Cast off!" Then he turned back. "Penelope, sing a shanty to get the men working on unfurling the sails."

Penelope sang the rest of the watch, as they negotiated the harbor and ran out to sea. Later, lying on her bunk, she thought about her change of fortune. By now, she had learned to like cooking, and that gave her real hope that she would enjoy the shanty man's job, too. She'd taken a job she hated at first and learned to do it with skill and joy. What could she do with a job she initially liked?

She was hoarse the first days of leading and singing shanties, but her voice soon settled into the sailing life, like a horse getting used to the bit. Her favorite pastime was flipping through her journals, looking for new shanties to try.

FEBRUARY. DOUGLAS, ISLE OF MAN.

Within two days, the *Hallowe'en* anchored off the shore of Douglas, the capital of the Isle of Man. The small island lay in the center of the Irish Sea, equidistant from England, Scotland and Ireland. Frenchie rowed Santiago ashore.

Santiago followed the detective's directions until he found Widow Nichols' white cottage on a wind-swept cliff overlooking the harbor. She wore black as did her three sons. Their clothing was worn and too small, but the boys spoke bravely.

"If you knew our father, you are welcome here," the oldest said. His back was straight and his eye clear, like his father's had been.

"I've come because I wonder if you might sell me a map he had," Santiago said.

Eagerly, Widow Nichols pulled out her late husband's sea chest. "We have no use for these things." She left unsaid what was obvious; she needed cash to keep her sons fed and clothed.

Captain Nichols had twenty maps, including the sea serpent map. Santiago let her bargain a price of 25 gold coins for the lot. Eagerly, she held up a pearl-inlaid telescope. "Would you be needing something like this?"

Santiago bought it for Penelope for five more gold coins.

"You're a real blessing," Widow Nichols cried. She insisted he stay to afternoon tea and tell her sons stories of life at sea before he left.

Back at the *Hallowe'en*, Santiago studied the sea serpent map. It was a forgery, he told Captain Kingsley. The fourth, in the hands of Captain Brice of the *Endurance*, was their only hope of finding the original. So, in spite of the late November weather, the *Hallowe'en* set sail across the northern Atlantic, bound for Boston Harbor. Captain Kingsley wanted that fourth map.

MARCH. CROSSING THE ATLANTIC, BOUND FOR BOSTON.

Penelope led the crew in an old song: "Oh, fare you well, we're homeward bound. We're homeward bound for Boston Town."

While the late winter weather was cold, Penelope and Santiago's conversations in their cabin were heated. Santiago told Penelope about Widow Nichols and how hard her life was. "We vowed," Santiago said, "to help those in need."

"Yes, but while we're crew members, we have to obey our Captain. There's not much chance of helping others."

"Not true." Santiago knelt on the bunk to stare out the tiny porthole. The north wind whipped the waves into white caps; it cut through the wooden hull, making their cabin feel almost Arctic. "I can't tell Captain Kingsley which sea serpent map is the real one without knowing what he plans to do with it."

Penelope shook her head. "You can't lie." They were in enough trouble from the lies about how she had secretly bought maps and how he had secretly copied maps.

"But I can't give him the sea serpent map if it means he'll hurt the creatures."

"We suspect him of lots. But do we really know what he plans?"

Santiago said, "The Captain's collection. You said before that it has something to do with all this."

Penelope sucked in a breath. She sat beside him on the bunk and whispered, "You want to see inside his secret room."

"We have to."

Penelope knew he was right.

They watched and waited for an opportunity. One night, after the Captain's mess, the third mate suggested a game of cards. For the first hour, the Captain won. This put him in such a good mood, he ordered Santiago to find some Spanish chocolate to celebrate; he gave Santiago his ship's keys and told him in which locker to look.

Realizing this was his chance, Santiago quickly found the chocolate. Then he stopped at his cabin and found candle stubs. Most of the keys, he recognized, but there were three he hadn't seen before. He pressed each key into its own bit of candle wax. When they reached Boston, he would find a locksmith and have keys made.

Coming out of his cabin into the dim passageway, Frenchie startled Santiago: "Where 'ave you been? Zee Captain's waiting."

"Sorry, sir." Santiago juggled the tin of chocolate and keys, and dropped the key ring. Leaning over, Santiago saw a bit of wax stuck to one of the keys.

"Give me zat." Frenchie reached for them.

Santiago juggled everything again, this time dropping the chocolate. While Frenchie picked up the tin, Santiago rubbed the keys against his pants leg, and then held them out for Frenchie. Would the penguin notice the wax?

Frenchie grabbed them and shoved the chocolate tin at Santiago.

"'Urry up," Frenchie said.

With shaking hands, Santiago followed him to the Captain's cabin. Though he was short on breath the rest of the evening, Santiago was confident Frenchie hadn't noticed anything. And they had what they needed to get into the secret room.

APRIL. TEN MILES OUT FROM BOSTON.

In spite of spring storms, they made good time crossing the Atlantic. By mid-April, excitement built as they neared Boston; for many of the sailors, it was their homeport. But ten miles out from the harbor, they met a schooner that told them the *Endurance* wasn't in harbor. She had wintered over, they said, in St. George's, Bermuda.

Captain Kingsley refused to put in at Boston; instead, he turned the *Hallowe'en* south.

APRIL. HEADING SOUTH FOR BERMUDA.

Penelope had braved the harsh spring winds for six weeks by telling herself she would soon see familiar shores. She focused her telescope on a distant lighthouse and wept as they left the coast of Massachusetts behind. She wanted to see Cricket and eat at the Tea Party Inn and walk on land for days and days.

She loved sailing, but homesickness almost overwhelmed her.

Alone in the stern, she sang softly as land disappeared, "We're homeward bound for Boston Town. Hurrah, my boys, we're homeward bound."

But there was nothing she could do but turn her face toward the south.

MAY. BERMUDA.

The fishhook-shaped islands were a tropical paradise: turquoise water, white sands, and exotic flowers blooming everywhere. St. George's was a prosperous city on the most northeasterly island, where waters were deep enough for a good harbor.

As soon as they docked, Captain Kingsley strode around the harbor searching for the *Endurance*. Luckily, it was still in St. George's.

Captain Brice still wore her curly hair short, tucked up under her captain's hat. Her boat was small and slow, but tough like its Captain.

When he stood on the dock, Captain Kingsley was twice her height, but Captain Brice puffed out her chest and refused to back down. "You offered me the *Hallowe'en*, and then took her away. I've no reason to help you. And I don't care if it's a forgery or not."

Santiago tried to reason with her. "Could I just look at it and compare it with the other three maps? One of them is real, but I don't know which one."

"Get off my boat," she roared. "It's my own map, and I'll not let the likes of you look at it."

Captain Kingsley and Santiago paced the docks in front of the *Endurance* until Penelope offered to try. "But I'll do it my way," she said.

They agreed.

"Don't take too long," Captain Kingsley warned darkly. "There are ways to make people cooperate."

For three nights, Penelope took her Irish harp into the taverns and sang the sea shanties and ballads she had learned in Dublin. On the fourth night, Captain Brice came to listen; on the fifth night, she sang along.

Afterwards, she roared her approval. "To hear a well-played Irish harp—ah, now that's worth a pretty penny."

She offered to buy drinks for Penelope—a rare thing for Captain Brice who was usually stingy with her copper, much less her silver.

While Penelope was wooing the Irish captain, Santiago located a secretive locksmith; he took the wax impressions and paid the right bribes. A day later, Santiago had three brass keys.

Meanwhile, the unlikely friendship between Captain Brice and Penelope grew. Penelope enjoyed the rough Captain's storytelling, and the Captain listened eagerly to Penelope's songs of Ireland. On the sixth night, Penelope came home with the map.

"She made me pay 50 gold coins for it," Penelope told Captain Kingsley. "She knew I'd bring it to you and wanted you to pay dearly."

"Foolish pig! I told you ten, and that's all you'll get." At a nod from the polar bear, Frenchie disappeared for a few minutes, and then returned with a leather pouch full of coins, which he dropped into her hands.

Penelope glared at Captain Kingsley's and Frenchie's clawed feet, knowing that if she looked up, she would say things she'd regret. Frenchie's claws had an almost reptile texture and were horizontally striped. Captain Kingsley's were just a dark shiny brown which shone in the midst of his yellow-white fur. They were stronger than Penelope and more likely to fight than she. She sighed in anger; she wasn't a ship's captain like Captain Brice, so she couldn't force him to pay the 50 gold coins. It meant she and Santiago would have to sell even more maps to get ahead.

Santiago spread out the four maps. Even at a glance, it was easy to see which map was the original; but he had to decide what to tell Captain Kingsley.

He bought time. "I need to study these with a magnifying glass to be sure. I'll have an answer by morning."

Captain Kingsley rocked back and forth on his large feet. Obviously, he didn't like this, but he had to trust Santiago's judgment. "By morning, then."

Santiago took the rolled maps to his cabin. Every inch of wall and ceiling space of fourth mate's cabin was covered with maps. The Talberts' small locker was full of Penelope's journals that held sea serpent stories or sea shanties. Penelope could understand the passion to collect. But what did Captain Kingsley collect?

15

SEA SERPENTS

The crew jostled for positions at the deck railing and called to those passing their ship. A jumble of languages met them as it did in every busy seaport.

"When can we go ashore, Frenchie, sir?" Cactus asked. "It's dusk already."

Just then, Captain Kingsley appeared in his dress uniform, the brass buttons polished until they glowed in the lantern light.

"Captain on-deck," Frenchie called and everyone snapped to attention. "Before you go ashore, I need a volunteer to stand zee watch."

Penelope sighed. She was longing for a stroll on dry ground as much as the others. "Sir, I'll do it. Santiago has to study the maps anyway."

Frenchie nodded to the crew. "Go. Report back in zee morning."

With whoops, they clattered down the gangplank and scattered. St. George's offered a variety of entertainment, and the crew—who had been paid that afternoon—had money to spend. Captain Kingsley and Frenchie were the last to disembark; they were invited to dine with the harbormaster that night, and afterwards they would visit a few taverns. Penelope and Santiago pulled up the gangplank, so it would be easier to stand guard.

Santiago rolled out the sea serpent maps on the table in the galley. The tiny room smelled of onions and garlic, the basis of everything Cactus cooked, but it had good lanterns to read by.

He held the magnifying glass over the first map. "I'll just pretend to study this a bit, in case anyone is watching. You can make the rounds of the deck. We won't do anything for a while."

Penelope walked slowly around the deck. Around the harbor glowed lanterns of other boats; in the dim light, figureheads loomed as giants. It was odd, Penelope thought, that the *Hallowe'en* didn't have a figurehead. Perhaps Captain Kingsley didn't like that old saying: the captain is the part of the ship that does the talking while the figurehead does the thinking.

Music, a dancing jig, floated over the water, and again Penelope longed to be off the boat. Well, one more night wouldn't matter.

Clouds drifted in and covered the moon and stars. Sometime before midnight a cool tropical rain drenched the boat. If it ran true to form, it would rain hard for an hour or two, and then blow over. Penelope made the rounds of the deck again, and came back to the galley soaking wet.

"Now. While it's raining," she whispered. "No one is out at this hour."

They took the keys from their hiding place under their mattress and tiptoed to Captain Kingsley's cabin. "We're dripping water everywhere," Penelope complained. "He'll know we were here."

She found a mop and swabbed the entire corridor, while Santiago changed to dry clothes; he waited while she changed, too.

They opened the door to the Captain's cabin. It was pitch black, with no light coming from the porthole, either. Santiago lit a small candle and quickly covered the round window with a cloth he'd brought. At the light, the Captain's parrot squawked, "Captain, Captain, Captain." He flew up in a whirr of green.

"Close the door! He can't escape," Santiago yelled.

Reacting instinctively, Penelope slammed the door. She winced at the noise, which echoed through the empty ship.

The parrot flapped around Penelope's head, trying to peck her. "Captain, Captain, Captain."

"Get away!"

Santiago grabbed a blanket from Captain Kingsley's bed and threw it over the bird; as the heavy blanket fell, it trapped the parrot. Carefully, Santiago picked up the bird—still wrapped in the blanket—and shoved it into the birdcage. He left the blanket draped over the cage.

Silence. Back in the dark, the parrot was quiet.

Santiago hardly dared breath. He whispered, "Did he hurt you?"

Penelope shook her head.

"Should we check the deck?"

"It's hard to board with the gangplank pulled up," Penelope whispered back. She cleared her throat; why were they whispering? "No one is out at this hour," she repeated loudly.

Santiago turned to the ebony door behind the desk. "Oh! I've left the keys in my other clothes. I'll be right back."

To Penelope, it seemed to take hours before he returned. She paced, three steps in one direction, reverse, three steps back, reverse, three more. "We're taking too much time," Penelope said, when he finally arrived.

Santiago whispered, "I think I heard something on deck."

"No," Penelope said with more assurance than she felt. "Relax. No one will be here until dawn."

With nerves jangling, they tried the door. The first key—a small, thin one—didn't fit. Feeling the keyhole, Penelope tried the largest key next. Too big. She held up the last key. "It's this or nothing."

Santiago held the candle close to the lock. The key turned silently: the door swung smoothly outward.

Santiago entered the secret room first, with Penelope right behind. Long and narrow, the room was really just a corridor that ran between shelves, a storage room. Each shelf held labeled glass jars. Penelope held the candle higher. The light fluttered, like Penelope and Santiago's heartbeats. A faint chemical smell lingered in the air. The sharp odor had to be formaldehyde, a colorless chemical liquid used to preserve things.

The thick greenish glass was hard to see through. Penelope moved the candle close enough to read a label and see the contents clearly.

Giant squid: a huge tentacle lay coiled in the jar.

Narwhale: a long horn sat diagonally in the jar.

Peruvian pyricthacanth: the head of the big-mouthed fish.

Oarfish, *Cadborsaurus*, Hydra, Monster Hagfish, *Morgawr*, *Morag*, Malaysian Dragon—the jars went on and on.

"A trophy hunter," Penelope croaked.

Captain Kingsley hunted rare marine creatures, and when he found them, he killed them and kept them as a trophy.

Horror held Penelope in its grip as she looked from one jar to the next. When it changed to anger, she walked slowly, touching each jar, making a vow with each touch that this collection wouldn't be tolerated. This was a betrayal of everything it meant to be an intelligent creature. When you treated another creature as a beast, it brought out the beast in yourself.

Of course that impulse—to exalt yourself and treat others as nothing—squirmed within every intelligent creature. The only thing that separated Captain Kingsley and Frenchie from Penelope herself was that they gave in to temptation. Some might deny it was there, but Penelope knew her heart.

Maybe there was something fundamentally different, though. Because Penelope held the fierce conviction that each creature was unique. Each "specimen" in the hideous glass jars had been special while living; dead, treated as just another specimen, they were an abomination. Captain Kingsley's collection wasn't just illegal: it was immoral.

Amidst the shelves, Santiago wept. "I should smash every single jar."

"Zat would be a mistake."

The Talberts spun around. In the doorway stood Frenchie.

"I wondered when you'd 'ave keys made from zee wax impressions you did." Frenchie tapped a webbed foot. "I wondered if you would 'ave zee guts to use zee keys." Excitement exaggerated his French accent.

In anguish, Penelope asked, "Why collect sea creatures like this?"

"We didn't mean to," Frenchie said. "Did we, Captain?"

The polar bear loomed in the doorway, filling the small corridor with his bulk. Penelope backed into Santiago, and together they backed away from the Captain. Both Frenchie and the Captain were dripping water onto the floor.

Penelope wasn't the only one who would view the collection as immoral, she was sure. If word got out about the collection, it would ruin the Ice King's business. Now that they knew his secret, he wouldn't let them go easily. "You're serpents!" she cried.

"No. We're collectors," Captain Kingsley said calmly. "It started accidentally when we found the Patagonian treasure." He lifted a jar down, unscrewed it and pulled out the long narwhale horn. "The unicorn of the sea, they call this. It was in the treasure chest." He shrugged his massive shoulders. "It started everything."

"First, a narwhale 'orn. Next, a giant squid tentacle. It just grew," Frenchie said. He held up his own candle and reached out a wing to touch a jar, as if he were touching something sacred.

"We are very close to having a complete collection," Captain Kingsley said.

Penelope heard the pride in his voice, heard the threat.

"And you'll help us. We only need one thing to complete our collection," Captain Kingsley said.

Frenchie stopped at the only empty jar. Reverently, he read the label: "Bermuda Triangle Sea Serpent."

"A sea serpent won't fit in that!" Penelope objected.

"A baby might. Or just its skull would do, you know," Captain Kingsley said. He unscrewed the jar, stuck his massive paw inside the wide mouthed jar and made a fist. He pulled his fist out and held it in Penelope's face. "There's room for an adult skull."

A sudden vision of jars with pigs' feet made her stomach heave. "You're mad!" she cried. "You kill intelligent creatures."

"Penelope!" Santiago warned. "You're making the Captain and Frenchie angry."

"No, no," Frenchie said. "Let me explain. When I was a chick, I was captured and sold to zee Paris Zoo. People came to watch zee trained penguin do 'is tricks. Zey poked and prodded me; zey zrew me peanuts as a treat. Zey treated me like an animal instead of an intelligent creature. You know what it's like; we all came from places where most animals were just animals. Something set us apart, zough. For some reason, we were born with intelligence zat our brothers and sisters weren't. Zee Captain and I know zee difference between animals and intelligent animals. What we collect are animals."

"How did you escape from the zoo?" Penelope asked. It was a good idea to keep Frenchie talking.

"I 'ad 'hard of zee Wide World from the birds," Frenchie said, "One day, I just walked out of ze Zoo. It was zat easy. Eventually, I found my way to zee Wide World. It was easy to find in France. At first, all I could zink of was returning to zee Antarctic. I took passage on a ship and went 'ome. But, zee Guardians wouldn't let me cross back to my 'ome."

Penelope understood this. If they went back to the pigsty, they couldn't stand it. They would try to change that world.

"I signed on to zee *Alaska* and met zee Captain. Zee rest you know."

"And what are we going to do with you now?" Captain Kingsley asked.

"I zink," Frenchie said slowly, "zey are part of our collection, for now."

Captain Kingsley gave a short laugh. "Not them. I only collect things that keep me awake at night. We'll have to think of something else."

Frenchie shrugged. "For now, zey will 'ave to stay 'ere."

Behind Santiago's back, Penelope silently unscrewed two jar lids.

"You're right," Captain Kingsley said. "They'll have to stay here."

"No!" With one quick motion, Penelope grabbed the first jar, shoved Santiago's head out of the way, and threw the contents at Captain Kingsley's eyes. Before Frenchie could react, she'd thrown a jarful at his face, too.

Instantly, formaldehyde choked everyone, sending Penelope into a coughing fit.

"Don't breathe," Penelope yelled at Santiago. They pushed past Frenchie and Captain Kingsley, who were rolling on the floor, clawing at their eyes.

Still coughing, the pigs rushed out of the Captain's cabin.

"This way," Santiago called. He raced toward their cabin.

"No. The deck is this way. We've got to get away," Penelope cried.

"I won't leave those maps for the Captain." Santiago's voice was grim and determined.

Penelope turned back with him. At their cabin, they jammed maps and journals into two duffle bags and, as they were leaving, Penelope caught up her Irish harp. They scurried up to the deck.

Frenchie and Captain Kingsley staggered up the opposite ladder, but they ignored the pigs. Instead, they crawled on all fours to the side of the boat and rolled over, into the water, to wash off the chemicals.

The Talberts shoved out the gangplank and pounded down. They plunged into dark alleys and side streets at random, sprinting away from the harbor. Their duffels banged against their backs, and Penelope got a stitch in her side, but they kept going. Finally, they stopped in the dark shadows of a house.

Penelope waited until she stopped panting. She whispered, "Do you realize what we've done?"

The storm was blowing over by now, and the moon reappeared from behind a lingering cloudbank.

Santiago nodded, "I couldn't give him the maps. Three are forgeries. If you have all of them, though, you can figure out the positions of the sea serpent island. I was exact in moving the island's position in each map. If you chart all three, it makes a triangle, and the island is in the exact center of that triangle. The original would only confirm that."

"Oh!" Penelope couldn't stand the thought of the Captain finding the island. "He'll kill a sea serpent just for his collection."

"Yes. And somehow, I don't think he'll leave the rest of them alone. He'll destroy every sea serpent on that island."

Penelope lifted her arm and smelled her shirt; formaldehyde still clung to her clothes. She shivered. "We can't take the maps back. Where will we go?"

Santiago leaned against the house and slid down to the ground. His head slumped onto his chest in despair. "He'll never stop hunting us. Never."

16

STORM AT SEA

Eighteen months later, Penelope was strolling along a rocky beach in Maine. Though it was summer, a cool breeze blew. She reached the rocky point of land, well away from the pines, and stopped to hold her pearl-inlaid telescope to her eye, the one Santiago had bought from Captain Nichol's widow. For a moment she blinked, unable to focus, fondly remembering the telescope joke that Odd had played on her and Santiago. But there was no going back to that life. Captain Kingsley would have them hanging from a yardarm if he caught them; for now, they were fugitives.

She turned the telescope to the south. There. White sails against the blue sky. Cricket's boat, the *Mercator*.

She ran back to the cove and yelled for Santiago. "She's here."

He came out of a tiny cabin hidden amidst the pines and waved at her. They watched for ten minutes while the boat maneuvered into the cove.

At last, Cricket jumped down barefoot, with her cotton trousers rolled up and her braid swinging into the salt water behind her; she waded noisily toward shore. Penelope splashed out to meet her, and they hugged and cried and laughed, all at the same time; Santiago waited onshore, but was ready with a hug, too, when Cricket reached him.

It was a joyous reunion. Over corn chowder, the Talberts told about their travels for the past eighteen months on their tiny yacht, the *Liberty*. They had bought her in Maryland last year, after Captain Brice had smuggled them out of Bermuda. The yacht had proven her seaworthiness, and then some, this year as they sailed around the world. Penelope's only regret was that she had left her journals and her Irish harp in the safekeeping of Captain Brice, taking only Santiago's maps and their duffels of clothing. She had thought that living in a small boat would be too crowded. Amazingly, though, the space was so well planned that everything had a snug place. She could have brought everything if she'd known. Some day, they would have to find the good Captain to get her things back.

Cricket, in return, told them the gossip from Boston Harbor: who was hauling what, where, and who had become captain of their own boats. Her map store, she said, had doubled in size, and she now had two apprentices.

Finally, she had disturbing news. She pushed back from the rustic table and went to stand in the open doorway of the cabin. The late afternoon sun sent spiky dark shadows from the pines reaching toward the *Mercator*. "Captain Kingsley was in again last week asking about you."

Penelope drew a deep breath. "He'll never give up. Never."

"I can't stay the night," Cricket said. "Kingsley knows I'm going to the Hildebrand farm in Maine and that I go there every year for paper. I suspect I'll find Frenchie waiting at that dock for me."

"He's followed you?" Santiago looked up sharply.

Penelope stepped outside the cabin with her telescope and swept the horizon. No sails, but that meant nothing. Anyone following Cricket would be discreet. Had someone followed her?

"Not here. I'm a better sailor than he is," Cricket said with a grin. "But I need to move on within the hour, or he'll overtake me. Be warned: that penguin is skulking about. I heard Captain Kingsley say they'll sail across the Atlantic to the Canary Islands next. Go a different direction. Stay lost."

Penelope swallowed hard. The Oriental woman was their oldest, most loyal friend. She was right: they'd never be able to let their guard down.

To cover her emotions, Penelope said, "I brought you something." From a shelf, she took a package and handed it to Cricket.

Cricket ripped off the brown paper. It was a new silk jacket.

"The latest style from Peking," Penelope said.

Cricket donned the turquoise jacket and danced a jig with Penelope while they both laughed with the joy of friendship. Penelope hadn't realized how much a visit with Cricket meant to her.

When they calmed a bit, Santiago said, "You'd better look at maps now."

They spent most of the remaining time looking at the nearly 100 maps he had bought for Cricket. In the past year, they had sailed in places away from the major shipping lanes. They had seen the Mediterranean Sea, the Black Sea, the South China Sea and many other seas. These neglected byways had brought them a surprisingly rich store of maps.

"These are marvelous," Cricket finally said. "I can double the price you paid on almost every one. I can pay you 500 gold coins for the lot."

"Enough to sail another year," Santiago said. That was all they needed just then. "Next year, the second week of July?"

"Yes. I'll be here," Cricket said.

After Cricket sailed away, the Talberts pulled the *Liberty* out of hiding. She was a white wooden sailboat with teak decks they had re-varnished while waiting for Cricket to arrive. They kept her in tip-top shape, and she repaid them with surprising speed for her size. She had only a mainsail, and it was well rigged, so they seldom had to climb aloft. The *Liberty* was, in fact, a joy to sail. Since Captain Kingsley was sailing east to the Canaries, they decided to sail south.

Maybe successfully hiding from Captain Kingsley for over a year had made them overconfident. Or maybe they were just getting tired of running. Either way, the pigs didn't notice a small sailboat hiding in a cove a mile down the coast, didn't notice when it slipped in behind them, didn't notice when it stayed on the horizon—now in view, now just out of view—while they sailed south.

They gave Boston a wide berth, but then hugged the coastline, taking time, here and there, to pull into likely coves and rest for a day. One night they tied up in a cove and were delighted to see a small river emptying into the ocean there.

"How long has it been since we had freshwater fish?" Penelope said. "Let's walk upstream and catch a few."

"Do you think it's safe?"

"We haven't seen anyone following us," Penelope said. "Captain Kingsley is halfway across the Atlantic by now."

They took their time strolling the riverbank, fly fishing and enjoying a rare day off the boat. They built a fire and roasted their catch for supper. Then they lay beside the fire on their backs and counted meteorites streaking across the sky. Finally, at midnight, they stumbled sleepily back to the *Liberty*, tumbled into their bunks, and slept.

Their bellies were so full of fish, their eyes so full of stars, they didn't notice someone had been on their boat. Someone with stealthy webbed feet had climbed onto the deck, had opened cabinets until he found the tubes with maps, had searched the maps until he found three skillful forgeries and one original—did he know the difference?—and had taken those maps back to his friend and master.

Because they didn't notice the quiet theft, the Talberts sailed happily the next day, continuing south to avoid Captain Kingsley. When they came to Florida a few weeks later, they decided to put out 100 miles or so to sea, to avoid the shipping and tourist traffic.

The sea around them changed; great clumps of seaweed, ripped free from some distant bed, washed past them. Schools of jellyfish floated by. Somehow the air was wrong; it was too warm, too humid, too calm.

"There's a big storm out there somewhere," Penelope said.

"Then we need to get back to shore before it catches us."

They sailed southwest, hoping to get around Florida, into the Gulf of Mexico, before the storm hit. But the clouds gathered quickly, and the winds rose against them. They tightened all the hatches and made the *Liberty* as watertight as possible. They strapped themselves into harnesses that were tied with long ropes to the mast; if they accidentally got swept overboard by a large wave, they wouldn't be lost at sea.

The small yacht flew over the waves, westward toward shore, running in front of the storm.

"Ship, ahoy!" Penelope pointed north toward a large sailing ship that was bearing down on them. Suddenly, her legs turned to jelly. "It's the *Hallowe'en*," she yelled over the storm's roar.

"She's supposed to be on the other side of the Atlantic. How'd she find us?" Santiago's voice was worried.

They both knew Captain Kingsley would be ruthless when he caught them. She remembered the vision she'd had before: black pig's feet inside a green glass jar. They were already running with full sail; they wouldn't be able to escape.

A wave caught the *Hallowe'en* broadside; they saw the white bulk of Captain Kingsley spinning the great wheel, so the boat lined up with the wave better. It was now between them and the storm. Oddly, he spun the wheel again and turned until he was facing into the storm.

"What's he doing?" Santiago cried.

The *Hallowe'en* disappeared behind the next wave.

"Why isn't he chasing us?" Then, Penelope knew. She threw open the hatch and plunged into the cabin. Frantically, she tore open the cabinet with the maps and raked through them. Gone. The sea serpent maps were gone. Penelope's throat felt tight. The mere possibility that Captain Kingsley would injure a sea serpent made Liberty suddenly narrow.

She raced back on deck. "He just wanted us to know. He's got all four maps. Somehow, he stole the maps from us." It could have been any of several nights when they'd been lax with security and taken a stroll or gone fishing. They had been too complacent.

A large wave threatened to crash onto the pig's boat, but instead, the faithful *Liberty* leapt to the wave's crest.

"We've got to stop him." Penelope and Santiago said at the same time.

The full fury of the storm overtook both sailing boats, and the *Hallowe'en* struck half their sails; the pigs, however, refused to lower even a square inch of sail. For a day, they chased Captain Kingsley, just managing to glimpse his boat or the boat's lanterns, in lulls in the storm. But there weren't many moments of calm.

Penelope worried: Would they survive the storm? Would Captain Kingsley find the sea serpent island? What would they do if they managed to catch up to the *Hallowe'en*? It was a fool's errand; they should turn tail and run. But she set her face into the wind and held the tiller steady, following the *Hallowe'en* as best she could in the roaring winds.

By morning, the storm did what they thought impossible: it worsened. A deafening wind tore at the sails until the pigs were forced to lower them or risk damaging the mast. The Talberts gave up worrying about the *Hallowe'en* because the

Liberty had to fight just to stay afloat. They were tossed at the mercy of the wind's will.

Just when they thought the boat would rip apart, another sight almost ripped their courage apart: coils rising, no, towering above their boat. As suddenly as they appeared, the coils were gone, but their boat was moving steadily against the wind; a sea serpent was pushing their boat against the waves.

Penelope thought about fear. The hound, back home on the farm, had caused her first and deepest fear, that she would be overwhelmed by cruelty. In Liberty, she'd learned dogs could vary widely and that cruelty could come from any direction. But she didn't believe cruelty would come from sea serpents, despite their fearsome appearance.

The boat halted with a jerk that threw Penelope and Santiago off their feet, caught only by their harnesses. The sea serpents had run them aground, Penelope thought. How else would they have found an island in the midst of this storm?

"Thank you," she called into the wind.

She spat out salty water, and then peered through the grey storm. Nearby, the *Hallowe'en* lay tilted on uneven ground, and, in the bow, like a giant figurehead, stood Captain Kingsley; his yellow-white fur was the only thing visible. He studied the waters around them. Frenchie staggered forward, fighting the wind, step by step, until he was beside his captain. He held up a whaler's harpoon, the weapon used to kill the huge creatures. It had a long, smooth shaft, tipped by an iron point with barbs to prevent it pulling out easily. Why did Captain Kingsley need it?

A sea serpent had just saved his ship by putting them aground. Sea serpents were definitely intelligent. The Captain had to know it; he'd heard Captain Eznick's story of rescue. Was he really going to attack those who rescued him?

Captain Kingsley's huge paws closed over the long harpoon. He hefted it, as if testing its balance. Then he lifted his nose to smell. A polar bear can smell a seal's breathing hole even if it is half a mile away and covered with three feet of snow. In the midst of the storm, he was hunting by smell instead of sight. Suddenly, he reared back his right arm.

"No!" Penelope shrieked.

Like an ancient Greek warrior throwing a javelin, the Captain hurled the harpoon. Over the storm's noise came a high-pitched squeal. The rope attached to the harpoon snaked out until the rope was taut; it was tied securely to the mast, and unless the victim dragged the entire *Hallowe'en* with it, it couldn't escape.

Dimly, through the thick curtains of rain, Penelope and Santiago saw coils; Captain Kingsley had hit a sea serpent.

There was a sudden lull in the storm. Without thinking, without consulting each other, they clambered off their boat and staggered across the slick, rain-soaked beach grass toward the *Hallowe'en*. When they reached her, they hauled themselves up the side of the boat. Santiago slipped and fell heavily onto his back; but he shook himself off and climbed again, until Penelope helped pull him onto the deck.

Everyone was below, out of the rain, except Frenchie and Captain Kingsley, and they only had eyes for the writhing coils in front of them. The sea serpent's squeals didn't stop, but undulated in heart-wrenching waves.

The pigs pulled knives from their belts and started hacking away at the harpoon's rope. Working as shanty man, Penelope had acquired an ear for the sound and an eye for the look of ropes in use. Three strands of fibers were twisted together for strength, making them hard to cut through; but taut against the wind, the ropes stretched to their limit and were easier to cut. As long as the sea serpent pulled against the rope, they had a chance of cutting through it before they were discovered. Still, the rope was at least as thick as their forelegs, so progress was slower than she liked. Penelope leaned into the work, putting so much weight on her knife hand, that a sudden jerk of the boat threw her off balance; she went sliding down the tilted deck, hitting the rails with a crash.

At the sound, Frenchie turned. With a bellow of anger, he dashed toward them, yelling, "All 'ands on deck! All 'ands on deck!"

Captain Kingsley saw them, too, but he turned back to the sea serpent and tried to haul the rope in by brute strength. He was pitted against a different sort of serpent, though; the rope didn't move.

Leaving Santiago to cut through the rope, Penelope leapt to meet Frenchie. The penguin was about her height, but she had the reach on him. She threw a right punch, her hooves connecting with Frenchie's jaw. He fell. But the crew was pouring onto deck from below.

Snap! The harpoon rope broke. The loose end thunked the deck, and then slithered away.

"No!" Captain Kingsley roared.

But the rope whistled through his paws, and he was left shaking them against the smart of a rope burn.

A fierce joy surged through Penelope; the sea serpent was free. She wished she could meet the sea serpent under different circumstances, when she might see the awful coils in a different light, might talk with the creature, might listen to the stories sea serpents told their children about sailing vessels. The creature was free, and that meant anything—anything!—was possible.

While the creature was escaping, though, the Talberts were being captured. Crewmen swarmed from under the deck toward them. Penelope put her back against Santiago's. They were surrounded by the *Hallowe'en*'s crew.

17

UNEXPECTED

Frenchie paced in front of the captives, Penelope and Santiago. His face was almost purple with rage. "You!" he yelled. "You 'elped zat serpent get away!"

The crew encircling the pigs was a scruffy looking bunch. Hair was plastered to their skulls, their striped shirts clung to their chest, and rain dripped from eyebrows, noses, ears. In short, they were miserable. The storm helped them in only one way: it carried away the stench of unwashed bodies, leaving only the clean smell of the ocean.

Captain Kingsley strode toward them. Though the deck was tilted and slippery and the wind gusted, he kept his sea legs.

Even above the roar of waves pounding the shore, Penelope and Santiago heard his deadly calm words: "What will we do with them? Eh, Frenchie?"

"String zem up," Frenchie said loud enough for everyone to hear.

Penelope turned, looking for a friendly face amongst the crew. But in the last twenty months or so, Captain Kingsley had replaced many crewmen. Cactus leaned against the galley door, his quills shedding rain like an umbrella. Penelope lifted her hooves to him in appeal, but he shook his head, and then went back inside.

She moved closer to Santiago, lifted her chin defiantly, and faced Captain Kingsley.

"You're accused of mutiny," Captain Kingsley said. "I gave you a direct order, and you disobeyed. As Captain of this boat, I am the law. You're guilty, and you'll hang."

In answer, the storm began to howl again, the wind tearing at the boat. A lantern ripped off and crashed at Captain Kingsley's feet. Oil sputtered and flared, but was quickly put out by the deluge. Meanwhile, the storm's wail escalated until nothing else could be heard. Cactus appeared in the galley doorway with a lantern; he stayed just inside the galley, out of the worst of the wind. The weak light only made the dark seem darker. Captain Kingsley shook a hairy paw at them, then pointed up toward the yardarm.

Despite the storm, he meant to hang them. Penelope shuddered. To think they'd come so far, only to wind up hung as traitors. It was almost unbearable.

Penelope glimpsed huge coils—were they green or brown?—in the midst of the rain. Suddenly, the boat lurched, and then tilted abruptly to the opposite side. The sea serpent had jolted the boat.

It happened so fast, that half the crew was thrown to the deck. Santiago fell heavily against Penelope and they rolled, crashing into the rails. Keeping his wits, Santiago heaved Penelope up, and they lurched over the side of the boat.

They landed in three feet of water, and another wave crashed over them. The water was rising, which had made the boat easier to tilt.

"Hurry," Penelope yelled.

The pigs raced toward their own boat. The wind pulsed in continuous gusts, pushing them back toward the *Hallowe'en*. But they managed to make slow progress.

The incoming waves had almost floated the *Liberty* because she was lighter than the *Hallowe'en* and hadn't been pushed so far onto shore.

When they reached her, they shoved hard, trying to lift her hull off the sand. Another wave helped pick her up and float her, but almost carried the boat away. Frantically, Penelope and Santiago grabbed the ropes hanging over the sides. They wrapped the ropes around their forelegs and put their hind legs against the boat's side. Little by little, they hauled themselves over and fell onto the deck. Penelope struggled into her protective harness, and then helped Santiago with his.

Already the *Liberty* was floating, carried by the awful, crashing waves. Captain Kingsley stood on the shore, braced against the wind, with one fist raised in anger. Frenchie was swimming, trying to reach them, but even the penguin couldn't make progress against the incoming waves.

Their boat was light, easy for strong waves to pick up, so they were swept out to sea. Penelope hoped the island wouldn't have any outlying reefs since they wouldn't be able to steer. More quickly than they thought possible, the island disappeared in the boundless grey sea.

Exhausted, Penelope and Santiago shrugged off the harnesses, went below, and closed the hatches. They crawled under the tightly tucked sheets of their bunk. The *Liberty* would either float or sink; nothing they could do would matter now.

Surprisingly, they slept, rocked by the violent storm.

When they awoke, the rocking had lessened. Coming on deck, they saw that the storm had quieted to a steady hard rain, and the waves, while still large, were manageable.

"We could raise sails now," Penelope said. "But where are we?"

"We were blown east off Florida," Santiago said. "The compass works, so I can steer west."

Like dull scissors, their bow hacked through the grey cloth of the sea. They had no idea of the location of the *Hallowe'en* or the sea serpent island. Clumps of seaweed clung to their hull, so Penelope had to lean over the bow several times that day to pull them off. Slowly the weather improved.

Calmer seas gave them time to talk about the sea serpent. "It saved our lives. Twice," Penelope said.

"Yes," Santiago agreed. "Do you think they've lost their home? Captain Kingsley will never leave them alone since he's found their island."

"I wonder how badly Captain Kingsley injured the sea serpent. I wish we could help them," she sighed.

When the weather cleared, Santiago was able to take navigation readings from the sun and stars. They were now west of Florida, into the Gulf of Mexico. They turned north and soon ran into the coast. They spent a pleasant day walking on the white sugar-sands, collecting shells kicked up by the storm. Penelope had a nice collection started of large shells.

Collections were odd things, Penelope thought. As a piglet, she had collected corncobs for a while. The corn crop had been ripe, and every slop bucket had cobs. She kept them lined up under a sty pole where her littermates wouldn't notice. But after she collected a couple dozen, the excitement of secret ownership had worn thin. She started playing with her collection; she kicked the cobs, rolled them, and chewed on them like a dog worrying a bone. She studied the different lengths, various diameters and differences between white and yellow corn. She invited her brothers and sisters to study the corncobs and choose their favorites. In short, she took pleasure in ownership, in playing with her collection and in sharing her collection. Captain Kingsley and Frenchie only cared about owning dead sea creatures. Penelope didn't understand the thrill of such a private, forbidden collection.

The next day, the Talberts sailed on, hugging the coastline and sailing north, then west past Mobile Bay, and towards the Mississippi River delta. Here they lingered in the warm bayous, hoping to hide from Captain Kingsley by doing something unexpected. One evening, the tide led them to a pleasant bayou where they tied up.

"We'll stay here a few days," Penelope said. "You can repair the sails while I fix everything else."

Santiago frowned. Sewing sails was the hardest task for their hooved feet. "No. You repair the sails, and I'll do everything else."

"It's your turn for sails."

"We can both work on the sails. It'll go faster that way."

With a sigh, Penelope agreed. But it would be an aggravating week for them both.

That first night, fog puddled over the bayou. Penelope and Santiago ate late and sang plaintive sea shanties far into the night. Penelope was in a pensive mood. Would they always be fugitives, hiding from Captain Kingsley? Santiago asked her to sing a few jigs, though, and the mood lightened.

At last, they decided to call it a night. They were climbing down the steps into the cabin for the night, when Penelope stopped.

"Shhh!" she said.

Santiago leaned forward to listen to the night.

Penelope whispered, "What is it?"

Santiago tiptoed back up the steps and onto the teak deck. The crying grew louder. Near the main mast, he found something wrapped in Spanish moss.

"What is it?" Penelope asked again.

"A baby." Santiago's voice was deep with wonder. "But I've never seen anything like it!"

The baby was obviously an intelligent creature. He had a snub nose, long body with short legs, and wide, searching eyes. When he batted his long lashes, he captured Penelope's heart.

"Here. Let me," she said, taking the bundle from Santiago.

Tacked to the mast, Santiago found a strange letter:

"Please help! My husband was lost in the storm,
and I am hurt.

Take my baby and sail with him
for a year and a day.
Then bring him back here to me.
Signed,
His Sick Mother"

Penelope studied the note. It was written in large block letters on a piece of ragged parchment. Maybe it had once had something else drawn on it, but it looked waterlogged and bleached by water and sun. Perhaps it had been on a ship that was wrecked and floated miles and miles before finding a shore on which to wash up. Most importantly, the parchment and the handwriting told them nothing about who had written the note. She re-read the strange letter.

"We can't take care of a baby for a year," Penelope cried. "No!" But the baby was warm and fit into her arms just right. She already knew that she would do anything to protect this child.

The baby started crying again: great wails filled the bayou. The still waters trembled at the sound, but wherever the mother was, she didn't appear.

Oh! He cried all night long. No matter what food Penelope offered or what lullabies Santiago sang, the baby just cried.

In the morning, bleary-eyed and yawning, they decided to search for the mother. They cast off. The boat began to rock, and the baby suddenly went to sleep.

"Keep sailing," Penelope whispered.

There were too many unanswered questions. What sort of creature was this baby? Why did the mother choose them to watch over the baby? Why a year and a day? What if they took the child and returned a year later, but no mother appeared? Still the baby's sleeping face was smooth and sweet.

"We were going to sew sails and mend the boat," Santiago said.

Penelope rubbed her cheek softly on the baby's forehead and smiled. "We'll be so busy with this baby that we'll have to stop at some port and buy new sails. And we'll let the sail maker rig them, too."

Santiago cleared his throat, and his face lit up with an answering smile. "You're right. We have to sail, so the child can sleep."

While Penelope tended the baby, Santiago hauled up the main sail, and they headed for open water.

18

A FULL LIFE

"Where should we sail for a year and a day?" Penelope wondered. They were still in the Gulf of Mexico, where the waters were relatively calm and deep blue.

"We'll stop by Bermuda," Santiago said, "and retrieve your journals and Irish harp. You need it to sing to the child."

"Too dangerous," Penelope said. "Captain Kingsley could have spies there."

Santiago shrugged. "Still."

Penelope knew what he meant; the thought of her harp made her smile, and she started humming an Irish lullaby. She missed singing shanties for the *Hallowe'en*'s crew—the only thing she missed about Captain Kingsley's ship.

"See? Hampshires have an ear for music," Santiago said.

"And Berkshires definitely don't," she teased.

"I can sing." He cleared his throat and sang, "La, la, la, la."

But Penelope didn't answer. She was remembering Captain Kingsley hefting the harpoon. "Seriously. Anywhere but Bermuda."

"You need your harp," Santiago insisted.

The baby started crying. He was lying in a hammock strung from the boom. Penelope went to pick him up and started singing a ballad. Her voice was almost hoarse from constant singing, because even sailing, only her singing would calm the baby. He cried constantly, like a baby with a colicky stomach. The interesting thing was how much he already understood. He spoke a few words. And he could already walk. Whatever kind of creature he was, he was maturing rapidly.

"We'll stop at a small harbor, not St. George's. I'll sneak over and find Captain Brice."

"We'll regret it," Penelope warned.

But they set course around Florida and out into the Atlantic towards Bermuda, 1000 miles away.

All the way, they argued about the advisability of stopping over. In the end, it was Dickens—for so they had named the child—who decided it for them. He wasn't eating well and was growing thin. Santiago insisted, "We've got to talk with a doctor."

"We don't even know what kind of creature he is," Penelope grouched. "How can a doctor help?" She watched the seagulls circling the mast, and her own worry circled endlessly; Captain Kingsley was looking for them, but Dickens was sick. Looking for them. Sick.

Sick. They had no choice.

Dickens sat in the stern, his dark eyes watching the waves thump gently on the boat's side. He had alligator-like hide, green or brown in color, depending on how the sun shone. His head was long and narrow; his legs were short and stumpy. Today, he looked greener, and Penelope wondered if that was partly because he was feeling poorly.

They sailed on fair winds into the Great Sound of Bermuda. The Bermuda Islands are shaped like a fishhook pointing southwest. St. George's is at the top of the hook, in the northeast. The hook itself encompasses the Great Sound, and at the bottom of the hook is the Port Royal Bay. Rather than taking a commercial mooring where they might be seen, they found a deserted cove and anchored.

Santiago waded ashore and walked north to the town of Hamilton. He came back a few hours later with a penguin, Dr. Kevlin.

The doctor climbed aboard and stopped abruptly when he saw Dickens. "What kind of creature is he?"

"We don't know," Penelope said. "We found him, and he obviously needed help."

"Where did you find him?"

"North," Penelope lied. She didn't like these questions. They only needed advice on how to take care of Dickens, not a meddler who would report them to Captain Kingsley.

The penguin bent over Dickens and examined his eyes and throat. He ran a flipper down Dickens' back. "His backbone's rough. I wonder if adults of his kind have a growth there."

Penelope struggled to unknot her stomach. She was anxious to figure out what was wrong with Dickens, but she also wanted this doctor to be gone, so they could leave.

After poking Dickens' stomach and asking him to walk around a bit, the doctor said, "I don't know what he is or what he eats, but my instinct says he needs fish." He shrugged up his flippers, and then let his head droop onto his chest to look Dickens in the eye. "Has he been swimming lately?"

Dickens shook his head.

"He's a baby," Penelope said. "He won't know how to swim. We've been very careful to make sure he doesn't fall into the water."

Dr. Kevlin lifted his head and glared at her. "You don't even know what kind of creature he is. How can you say that?" To Dickens he said, "Go on. Jump in."

Penelope stamped a hoof and started to protest, but Dickens had already slid smoothly into the water. He didn't swim by moving sideways like a fish, but by undulating his short body, like a mermaid might.

Dr. Kevlin beamed. "He does swim."

Suddenly, Dickens dove and the water churned for a moment. When he appeared, he had a small fish in his mouth and was tearing it apart.

The penguin nodded. "Fish. Let him swim every day, and he'll catch his own. It's what my chicks would do. Penguins don't look like carnivores, but we are, you know. Feed me vegetarian stuff, and I'll get sick, too."

They watched Dickens playing in the cove. He ate two more fish, and then swam contentedly on his back with his eyes closed.

Penelope sighed with relief. She was wrong about Dickens swimming, and she didn't care, as long as he had more energy and gained weight. "Thank you, Doctor."

The breeze whispered through the tops of the palms.

Dr. Kevlin said quietly, "Someone has been looking for two black and white pigs."

"Hampshires or Berkshires," Santiago asked automatically.

"You're different breeds?"

Santiago carefully laid out the history of Berkshire pigs. "The Queen's breed, you know." But after the story, he asked, "Did you say your fee for tending the child is $25 in gold coins?"

"No. $50," Dr. Kevlin said.

Santiago barely held back his anger. $25 was a huge fee for a doctor, so he'd already offered extra for the penguin to keep his mouth shut. This penguin was asking for a huge bribe. "For $50," Santiago said, "you can tell us if Captain Brice and the *Endurance* are in St. George's harbor."

"They sailed three weeks ago."

Santiago paid the bribe for silence, while Penelope fumed.

After the penguin left, Penelope said, "We need to leave Bermuda immediately."

"It'll take Dr. Kevlin weeks to get a message to Frenchie or Captain Kingsley," Santiago said.

"Unless they're in St. George's."

"He took our gold," Santiago pointed out.

"That means nothing," Penelope said. "He could still tell, and we could do nothing. He just made $25 extra." She called to Dickens, "Come in, now."

Dickens swarmed up the rope easily, and then stood dripping onto the deck. Penelope scolded him and set him to work mopping up his mess.

When dusk fell, they set sail again, sailing north out of the Great Sound, then turned south to skirt the hook of the islands, and then headed east. While Santiago took the rudder, Penelope took Dickens downstairs into the cabin for his nap. While he twisted around on the bunk, she started straightening up. She had meant to work on the map cabinet for the last few weeks, so she pulled everything out and stacked them onto the tiny cabin table. She found one stack of maps that Santiago had bought from Captain Nichol's widow out of sympathy. They had forgotten to show them to Cricket and get her appraisal of them. They were clearly old. The parchment was yellowed, the edges frayed. Within the stack, Penelope spotted a darker map. She pulled it out, opened it and stared in wonder. The stained parchment spoke of age; the lettering–especially the odd spelling–spoke of days gone by.

"Dickens, look." Her heart thumped loudly in her ears.

But Dickens had settled down and gone to sleep. Penelope stroked his forehead with her hoof and smiled. The fish meal had done him good; this was the deepest sleep he'd had in several days. Penelope brushed his cheek with a kiss, then, by candlelight, she pored over the map.

It showed the Atlantic, but oddly distorted by expanding the east to west width. The sea serpent island was clearly marked, an astonishing thing in itself. There was another island shown, too: Atlantis, the lost island of legend. Of course, Atlantis was gone, if it had ever existed. But there were other, smaller, islands marked.

Penelope wondered how so many islands could be there and no one know about them. One especially intrigued her: it was a small island in the south Caribbean, near the equator, and out of the main shipping lanes. There was no reason for a boat to sail near that space of ocean unless they knew there was an island.

At last, Santiago tied down the sails for the night and came downstairs. Together, the Talberts studied the map.

Decidedly, Santiago said, "That's what we'll do this year. Explore these islands."

With the decision made, they slept well that night. The next morning, they turned south.

Dickens grew fat on a more varied diet. Within a couple weeks, he was running all over the deck, learning about sails, masts, sheeting lines, and anchors. In the evenings, Dickens learned to belt out sea shanties. His voice held a hint of whale songs, of tides that rise and fall and sweet rains upon the waves. As long as he sang, other creatures of the sea lingered beside the boat to listen.

Other evenings, Dickens learned to read and draw maps. He had four fingers, each ending in a claw; when he retracted his claws he could hold things much easier than the pig's hooves. He loved to play with Santiago's pencils and paints. He had a flair for decorating the maps with compass roses and coils of sea serpents.

"If you continue getting better at mapmaking," Santiago told him, "I'll ask Cricket if you can apprentice with her." Santiago had to remind himself, though, that Dickens wasn't his child. "If you want to," he added.

Then he told Dickens again of how they found him in the bayou and how they would take him back to find his mother at the end of a year and a day. Santiago could only repeat that they knew nothing about her except for her letter. It wasn't enough, but it was all Santiago could offer.

Dickens held the letter gently with his claws and read it over again. "A year and a day," he read. Then he sighed, folded the letter and went back to his mapmaking.

As a precaution, the Talberts sailed first to Barbados, off the coast of Venezuela. They docked there for a couple weeks, watching anxiously to make sure no one had followed them. Dickens was unhappy while they were onshore because he had to stay in the cabin. They didn't want to draw any extra attention by letting people see such a strange child. But Dickens was old enough now that he tried to have patience.

When Santiago was satisfied they weren't being watched, they sailed southeast, toward the islands on the Captain Nichol's map. They sailed slowly, doubled back often, zigzagged north and south, east and west. Penelope constantly scanned the horizon with her telescope. When she was finally satisfied no one had followed them, Santiago zeroed in on the first island.

At first, it was a dark smudge on the horizon; it grew to be a good-sized tropical island. Black sand beaches, salty marshes, a short mountain range and a forest at the mountain's foot—these made the island interesting. Penelope had worried that life on an island would be boring, but this one had variety. Even Dickens liked the island and called it Black Sands Island. He went off exploring for a couple hours at a time and always came back with something to show them: a bird's egg, a piece of driftwood, a coconut that they had to crack open for him. Later on, he dove into the protected lagoon and caught fish for supper. In the evening, they curled up on the warm beach and slept.

After a week on the island, Penelope slept late one morning. Yawning widely, she realized that she was completely relaxed, like she hadn't been in several years. The feeling surprised her. She hadn't realized how wearying it was to hide from Captain Kingsley, to constantly be on guard. She motioned for Santiago to sit beside her, and they watched Dickens fishing in the lagoon.

"Let's stay here," Penelope said. "We'll be safe for the year."

"No," Santiago said. "Let's try the other islands on the map."

Penelope was tired, though. Tired of exploring. Tired of pushing hard to do the next thing. Tired of always taking a risk. "Maybe we should've stayed on the farm," she said.

"You don't mean that!"

"Of course I don't mean it. But I'm always looking over my shoulder, always wondering when Captain Kingsley will find us." She pointed to the gulls flying overhead. "Is one of them a spy?" She stood angrily and strode down the beach, leaving deep hoof prints in the wet sand. Dickens was twenty feet off shore, eating his first fish of the morning. The turquoise blue waters allowed Dickens to easily see fish to catch and, at the same time, made it easy for Penelope to watch over Dickens. She liked easy for a change.

Santiago spun Penelope around and stood with his forelegs on her shoulders. "Penelope, don't you realize that life is a risk? We're not safe anywhere." He dropped his forelegs. "Oh, I know what you mean. There are places where the physical risks are fewer. But do you really want to stay in those places for long periods of time?"

"We stayed in Boston for a year."

"Because we both needed to learn about Liberty," Santiago said.

"We could stay here a year."

Santiago shook his head. "What does your heart tell you?"

What did her heart tell her? That it was safer to keep moving. She knew that they would settle down sometime. They had sailed the world and had many adventures; soon, they would start to slow down and think about starting a family. But not yet. For the year Dickens was with them, they need to keep moving. "I don't want to listen to my heart," she griped. "I want easy."

Dickens bounded out of the water and shook like a dog. "Why are you two fighting?"

Santiago motioned for Penelope to answer.

She studied Dickens. He had grown a foot—maybe two—already, and judging by his feet, it was clear that he would grow much, much larger. His hide today was a rich warm brown. He was inquisitive and intelligent. He forced her to think about everything from biology to astronomy and explain it in a simple way, while omitting none of the complexities of the world. She would never have known Dickens if they hadn't taken the risk of coming to Liberty, if they hadn't taken the risk of rescuing a helpless baby.

Life should get easier as it went along, but it didn't. They had taken many risks to get to Liberty, and once there, there had been more risks to get to Boston and to get a position on a ship. It should be getting easier. But the struggle remained the same: she could choose safety and a small life. Or she could risk everything on the chance that there was more out there. Safety was an illusion; clinging to it could make you miss the best things in life. She wanted—yes, she still wanted—a full life.

"We're trying to decide which island to visit next," Penelope told Dickens. "And I'm scared. We don't know what we'll find. But we're going to face the fears together, the three of us, and have an adventure."

"Hurrah!" Dickens yelled. "Adventure."

So, they climbed aboard the *Liberty* and sailed to another island, and then another.

One island especially remained in their hearts. It was another black-sand island, but smaller this time. The lagoon was particularly large and deep, and wide open to the ocean. They anchored that first night and went to sleep, Penelope, Santiago and Dickens nestled together in the cockpit. Penelope woke in the dark. Through the open hatch, she watched the mast swaying gently, sweeping the stars. Water lapped at the boat, rocking them on the ocean's breast.

Then she heard it again. It was a long, low melodic sound, and she recognized it at once: the song of the humpback whale. While the Ice King cut blocks of frozen water to ship world wide in the frozen north, the humpback whales were singing in the warm waters of the south Caribbean. The whale songs rose up out of the sea and filled the *Liberty*.

Penelope was aware that Dickens and Santiago were awake also, but it surprised her when Dickens rose and slid up to the deck. Before either pig knew what was happening, Dickens was in the water, swimming with a small pod of humpback whales. The whales' flippers slid over Dickens, examining him. Though he was longer and sleeker than the whales, they seemed to accept him. He tucked his legs tight against his body and glided in and out of the whales in a dance of celebration. Dickens sang with the whales, his quicker, lighter grace notes blending with their deep slow song. Now and then, a humpback breached or slapped his tail for added percussion. Penelope watched and listened until the beauty of the creatures and the song and the ocean and the stars filled her heart with joy.

It was for wonders like this that they had taken the risks needed to come to Liberty: Life was indeed full.

And so, they explored tropical islands for ten months. But the letter had asked them to bring Dickens home at the end of a year and a day. Dickens wasn't their child, Santiago reminded Penelope. They had to take him back to his mother.

As the end of the year drew near, Penelope began to worry about Dickens. He had grown into a long, sleek creature. His baby teeth were gone. In their place, new teeth were pushing up. Sharp new teeth.

"What kind of creature is he?" Penelope asked Santiago.

Dickens had taken to coiling himself around the mast for his afternoon naps.

"A one-of-a-kind," Santiago said. "A treasure."

Penelope nodded. "I love him, too."

Santiago put his foreleg around Penelope's shoulder, and they watched the moon rise. "What will happen to him when we get back?"

"Don't know," Santiago said, "Don't know."

Still, they had no choice, for he wasn't their child; they boarded the *Liberty*, unfurled the sails, and set a north western course.

19

HARPOON

One night, sailing back across the Caribbean, Dickens was singing shanties and ballads, as usual. It was dark, no moon. Only the smudge of the Milky Way reflecting off the water. There were phosphorescent algae in the water—the real thing, not a joke like Odds played on them so long ago. As always, Dickens' voice held a hint of whale songs, of tides that rise and fall, and sweet rains upon the waves. The algae heaved upwards and then settled quietly, as if disturbed by a whale. Penelope wondered what lurked under the water, but try as she might, she saw nothing.

"Tell me about my mother," Dickens asked for the hundredth time that day. He leaned over the railings and watched the deep waters.

Penelope watched, too, for the algae to heave again. As she had many times before, Penelope told about the letter they'd found with him, and their promise to deliver him back to the bayou where he'd been found. Dickens could recite the story from memory, but he still liked Penelope to tell it. "And the letter said to bring me back in a year and a day."

"Yes. That's only a month from now."

"Where is the bayou?"

"It's not on a map. We'll just have to find the place again."

"One month," Dickens repeated.

Although the weather had been pleasant, they hit a storm. The waves weren't particularly violent, or the wind particularly strong, or the rain particularly fierce, but somehow the combination of waves, wind and rain ripped off the hatch, and before they could get the latch fixed and the hatch back in place, their remaining flour, sugar, and coffee were soaked. They could eat fresh fish, but they needed fresh supplies.

"You know what this means?" Santiago warned.

"Bermuda," Penelope moaned. "It's closest." Somehow, they would have to hide Dickens while they made repairs and bought food.

Santiago nodded.

"We'll regret it," Penelope warned.

This time they decided to risk docking near St. George's. They could restock supplies quicker there and also look for Captain Brice. Penelope still wanted to retrieve her journals and harp. Because they were going to St. George's, they didn't enter the Great Sound again, but this time, they left Dickens on a tiny outlying island, which lay at the barb end of the fishhook formation. The island had fresh water, a good fishing cove, and lots of trees for cover.

"Whatever happens, don't come looking for us," Penelope said. "Promise."

"I'll be safe," Dickens said.

"We'll only be gone 24 hours," Santiago reassured him.

"I'm almost a year old," Dickens said indignantly. "I'll be fine."

The Talberts sailed to St. George's and tied up at a marina several miles away from the harbor. It was a busy marina meant for small sailboats like the *Liberty*; the sky bristled with masts. No one here, they hoped, would notice their comings or goings.

They ordered supplies and quickly loaded them. They waited until dark to walk to St. George's harbor. The late summer heat lingered, making the sands warm. Coming to the harbor so late meant most boats had their lanterns lit and a skeleton crew manning them. The air was heavy with the sweet smell of sugar canes, mingled with a fish smell. The Talberts were careful to stay out of the bright moonlight. If the *Endurance* was docked, they wouldn't risk going aboard, but look for Captain Brice in her favorite taverns.

Staying in the shadows, well away from the water, they edged around the harbor, looking more for the familiar shape of a schooner than for the names on the side of the boats. It was a busy season, and the harbor was full. Finally, they spied a schooner.

Santiago dropped to all fours and crept in close; when he scampered back a moment later, he was smiling. "It's the *Endurance*, all right."

They crept back to the shadows of a store before standing upright again. Just as they did, a paw clapped Santiago's back and spun him around.

"Well, look what we just found," Captain Kingsley said.

Penelope yelped in surprise, "No!"

Santiago shrugged off the paw and drew himself up, bravely. Though he was only half the height of Captain Kingsley, he was still a Berkshire boar in his prime. He would go down fighting. He threw the first punch, his hoof catching Captain Kingsley square in the stomach. The polar bear sagged for a moment, trying to catch his breath.

Penelope's own stomach went hollow; she didn't know if she was more scared before or after Santiago hit the Captain.

Thinking fast, she turned toward the *Endurance* and yelled to anyone who might hear her. "Find Captain Brice. Tell her Penelope needs help. Find Captain Brice." She didn't know if the watchmen on the *Endurance* would do as she asked. It was a slim hope, but they were desperate.

In a wild attempt at escape, Santiago shoved Penelope down an alley and followed her. Frenchie, his webbed feet flapping, chased them. Captain Kingsley made up for his slow reaction to being punched by pounding after them. With his long strides, he easily caught up to Santiago.

Penelope tried to scream, but terror left her speechless.

Captain Kingsley spun Santiago around; this time, the Captain hit Santiago with his open paw, which was as large as Santiago's head. It caught him square on, making Santiago topple like a broken mast.

Penelope surged toward Santiago, but stopped. She caught her breath. The Captain was advancing upon her. She lifted her fore-hooves, ready to strike, but he towered over her. She and Santiago were both lost.

Santiago, though, rolled towards the Captain, kicked out and got his hooves tangled in the Captain's feet. The polar bear tripped, waving his forelegs in a desperate attempt to stay upright. He landed with a tremendous thump.

With that, it was Frenchie who reached Penelope first, with a knife in his wing. He taunted her with it. "Where is zee sea serpent?" He tossed the knife from wing to wing. "We've 'eard rumors zis year. Zat you took aboard a strange foundling." He nodded at her look of dismay. "But we're patient. We've shadowed zee *Endurance* for seven months. Captain Kingsley was sure zat you'd try to see Captain Brice—sooner or later. What a boring seven months!"

The alley was dark, not well lit. The sugar and fish smell of the harbor was replaced by the smell of garbage, making Penelope almost gag. To fight was hopeless; Frenchie and Captain Kingsley were better fighters, more vicious and cruel. There would be no help, either. Alley fights among sailors were common, and seldom did anyone pay attention. She and Santiago were alone. Despair tasted bitter in her mouth.

On the ground, Captain Kingsley and Santiago were rolling; first the white polar bear was on top, and then the black and white pig. Penelope had no time to watch. She faced Frenchie squarely and watched his shoulders; if he was really going to slash her, the shoulders would tell her which direction to dodge. Though she had avoided most sailor fights, she had learned a lot by watching.

Frenchie stepped left, but his shoulders didn't move. Penelope leapt right, just a fraction of a second before he tried to slice her stomach. She bent, scooped up trash and flung it at Frenchie's face.

Startled, he jumped backwards.

It wasn't much of an opening, but she took it. She shoved past the penguin and untangled Santiago from Captain Kingsley. She thrust up her husband, and they raced for the street again. This time pursuit was slower. They found their way to the beach and raced toward the marina where they had left the *Liberty*.

Finally, the penguin appeared behind them. Where was Captain Kingsley? What was he planning?

The beach sand pulled at their feet as they ran. Penelope ran closer to the water, where the waves washed the sands, and gave a firmer surface. Frenchie didn't gain on them, but they didn't leave him behind either.

At the marina, they snatched the mooring ropes loose, leapt onto the *Liberty* and shoved off, leaving Frenchie standing on the dock. They unfurled the mainsail and turned to head out of the harbor. The wind hit Penelope's face, and the bow sang sweetly; they would soon be in the open waters, where nothing could catch their boat. Penelope's heart lifted.

But a sail hove into view, just outside the harbor: the *Hallowe'en*!

The large sailboat rounded the point and now stood blocking the mouth of the harbor. A rowboat shoved away from the point and soon pulled alongside the *Hallowe'en*. Captain Kingsley climbed aboard. He quickly strode to stand it the bow, glowering at the pigs' small sailboat.

Jerkily, Santiago dropped the sails. His black brow was furrowed with despair. "We were so close to getting away." He beat a hoof on the ship's wheel.

"What now?" Penelope asked.

But Santiago just shook his head. They were bottled up in this harbor, like Captain Kingsley bottled his gruesome trophies in the green jars.

Behind them, Frenchie untied a rowboat and jumped in. He rowed steadily until he reached the *Hallowe'en* and was taken aboard, too. For long minutes, the *Hallowe'en* and the *Liberty* faced each other in a stand off. It was a test of nerves, and Penelope felt like she was melting in the moonlight that glistened on the waves.

Santiago paced. Back and forth. He stopped and studied the *Hallowe'en*. She didn't move. Back and forth. Finally, Santiago said, "We've got to make a run for it." He drew close to Penelope to explain the details of his plan.

"Okay." Penelope's heart thumped loudly in her ears. It was a foolish plan, but they had to try something.

The pigs hauled the mainsail back up, and when the wind caught, they ran straight for the larger boat, as if they would ram her. Blessed by a stiff breeze, they surged faster and faster. At the last minute, Santiago executed a perfect 90-degree turn, and ran at right angles to the *Hallowe'en* until their stern was ten feet past her, before executing another perfect 90-degree turn back toward the open water.

"We made it," Penelope whispered. Did she dare hope?

Just as they skimmed past Captain Kingsley, the *Hallowe'en*'s cannons spoke. Boom! Boom! Boom! Cannon balls whizzed through the air.

"No!" Santiago cried.

Splash! Splash! Two cannon shots landed far short, but one—Crash!—caught the edge of the *Liberty*. Water poured into a small hole on the stern.

"We didn't make it." Penelope's despair made her voice crack.

"Man the pumps!"

Penelope jumped to the pump and started lifting and lowering the mechanism's handle, pumping water from the hold.

Santiago leaned over the tiller and tried to study the hole beneath him. From the hull, splintered wood jutted out.

"A big hole. It's bad!" he called. "Pump harder!"

Now, Santiago had to steer and handle the sails by himself. He was adept at this, but everything was slower with only one performing each task. For several minutes, each pig concentrated on his or her job.

Their momentum had indeed carried them past the *Hallowe'en* into the open water. The larger sailboat was turning to follow, but it maneuvered slower. They had a slim head start.

Would it be enough?

Penelope heaved at the pump harder, trying to lighten the *Liberty*. Finally, as the rhythm of the pumping took over, Penelope was able to look around. "Oh!" she cried. "Why'd you sail toward Dickens' island?"

Looking over her shoulder, she saw the *Hallowe'en*'s sails billowing out like great clouds. Captain Kingsley was giving chase.

Santiago sagged. "I wasn't thinking. I just headed away from the harbor. We'll sail past his island. We won't stop."

He shook his head. "This way, Dickens will know what's happening. Maybe it's better."

"Frenchie thinks that Dickens is a sea serpent," Penelope said.

"Of course."

And Penelope realized that he was right. She had known, perhaps from the first moment she saw him, that Dickens was a sea serpent baby. That his mother had been injured by Captain Kingsley's harpoon and had followed them through the storm. She just hadn't wanted to admit it, because she liked the small thrill of not knowing. But it was true: Dickens was a sea serpent. Captain Kingsley wouldn't rest until he found Dickens, the last thing needed for the collection. They had to lead him the other way.

Penelope dared not leave the pump unmanned; even with her pumping, she was afraid they were taking on too much water and would slowly sink. If they had time, they could rig a temporary patch, but neither of them could do it now. Somehow, they needed to leave Captain Kingsley far behind.

But as she watched, the Captain's boat gained on theirs.

When the line of islands came into sight, Santiago tacked and headed almost due north, seeking to avoid the outlying islands entirely. This was a mistake. The *Hallowe'en* moved to cut them off. Santiago tried to turn back and go south into the Great Sound.

Penelope's forelegs ached from pumping, but their boat was foundering now, too heavy with water; Captain Kingsley's boat was faster, and he cut off their retreat to the south. Santiago had to turn—the *Liberty* moved even more sluggish now—and slowly, surely, Captain Kingsley herded them into a cove of Dickens' island.

Captain Kingsley meant to send them aground, and then board them, Penelope realized.

She didn't want the Captain's huge paws thumping about on the teak deck that she had swabbed every day for the last two years. She didn't want him in her cabin, hunting for Dickens. She didn't want him within a mile of that sweet child. Yet, they had brought him straight to the island where Dickens was hiding. Despair made her weep.

Penelope stopped pumping and tried to help raise more sail. But it was too late.

Her jaw tightened. Dickens had to be safe.

Creaking and groaning, the *Liberty* ran into the shallows and foundered.

"Stay on board," bellowed Captain Kingsley to his crew. "This is our fight. Frenchie, let's go."

Before the pigs could do anything, Captain Kingsley swam the short distance to their boat. His huge paws clung to their railings, and he heaved himself over. On their tiny yacht, he looked like a beached whale.

Santiago pulled Penelope to the stern. "We have to swim for it."

The polar bear easily ripped open the cabin's door. Penelope felt her heart rip, too. The boat was her home, and he was tearing it apart.

But Santiago tugged at her again. "Swim!"

This time, she dove with him into the shallow water and waded ashore. At a splash, Penelope looked back. Frenchie was swimming toward them, his wedge-shaped body flying effortlessly through the water.

Penelope's thoughts swirled. *Dickens, stay safe!* she silently begged. *Stay hidden.*

Behind them, a roar erupted from their boat, and Captain Kingsley, glaring white in tropical moonlight, appeared, more enraged than ever. "Where is he?"

With a bound, the bear leapt into the water and waded after them. Frenchie pulled out of the water at the same time his captain did. He held two harpoons. He handed one to Captain Kingsley, and they came after the Talberts.

Though they ran, the pigs were easily overtaken again by the polar bear's longer strides. This time, he slapped Penelope with an open paw. Blinded with pain, she tumbled sideways and landed heavily. Santiago took a similar blow and fell beside her.

"Where is the sea serpent?" Captain Kingsley demanded. He straddled both of them.

Penelope blinked, trying to ignore the pain in her head, trying to erase the sight of the towering polar bear. Dully, she thought, *there's no escape.*

The waves slapped gently on the boats. Otherwise, the island was silent.

The Captain's face contorted into anger. He snarled, "Tell me." He reached for Penelope's legs as she lay on the sand. She kicked hard, but he grabbed her and jerked her upward. She hung upside down, swinging like a pendulum. Though her head swam with dizziness, the thought still pulsed through her: Stay safe, Dickens. Dickens. Safe.

Santiago roared with the frustration.

"Watch yourself," the Captain warned. His voice raged like a storm. "If you move, I'll swing her around and throw her against those trees."

Santiago froze in place, but his eyes never left Penelope as she swayed back and forth.

The pigs were utterly helpless.

The moon lit the beach with a warm glow. A calm descended on Penelope. So, this was how it ended. She had waited for Santiago in the moonlight, and he had come for her in the moonlight; they had moved into Liberty and learned to sail; they had lived a life of adventure. In this last adventure, she faced the hardest test. She needed to summon what courage she could because she must never tell the Captain where to find Dickens.

"Where's the serpent?" Captain Kingsley spoke into her ear.

Penelope said, "I'll never tell you."

The Captain's one good eye flared in anger. He lifted her high and swung her around in wide circles, until her body was flying straight out. She closed her eyes against the blurry, spinning world.

Suddenly, he stopped swinging her. Dizziness washed over Penelope anew.

Panting slightly, Captain Kingsley repeated. "Where's the serpent?"

It's been a full life, she thought.

Captain Kingsley lifted her again to swing her around. "No answer, eh? Maybe next time I'll let go, and you'll crash into those trees." He looked over at Santiago, who was now guarded by Frenchie. "You want to tell me where they are?"

Santiago shook his head. "No." His voice was tight with anger at the Captain and worry for Penelope.

"Then, here we go." Captain Kingsley heaved Penelope upward and took a step to start her spinning.

Suddenly, from the palm trees behind them, burst a whirlwind of sand and in the midst of the whirlwind, Penelope glimpsed coils. Dickens. No! Stay hidden, she wanted to call.

But before she knew what was happening, Penelope was snatched from the Captain's paws, and laid—gently—on the ground.

Over her, Dickens' wide eyes blinked back tears. "Penelope," he asked, "Did he hurt you?"

Penelope tried to smile at him, but couldn't. He didn't know what he'd done.

The Captain's face changed from anger to deep satisfaction. "At last," he whispered.

Frenchie whistled. "Our collection will be complete."

Captain Kingsley switched the harpoon from his left to right hand and reared back.

"No!" Penelope had risen to all fours and saw it coming. She charged desperately at Captain Kingsley. From the corner of her eye, she saw Santiago charging, too.

Captain Kingsley hurled the harpoon, just as the pigs struck at his knees. The polar bear toppled.

Pigs and bear—together, they rolled down the beach, into the water. For a moment, the pigs had the upper hand; the

Captain was stunned, and they were able to hold his head underwater. But he recovered himself, shook them off, and stood on all fours, shaking water from his fur and gasping for breath.

Something whistled in the air.

Penelope felt something strike her right shoulder. A harpoon stuck there. In wonder, she looked up and saw Frenchie at the edge of the water. He no longer held his harpoon. She staggered toward him. She stopped. The harpoon was heavy, somehow. She knocked at it with her forelegs, and it fell into the water. Dropping to all fours, she found it and picked it up. Why did she need it? Why did her shoulder hurt? She stood again, holding the harpoon.

Looking up, she saw Dickens on the beach with his coils in an untidy heap. He didn't move. A harpoon stuck out of his chest. Stupidly, she thought, now, *he'll have a scar. Why didn't he get up and show her?*

She looked at the thing in her hooves. Why did she hold a stick? Where was Santiago? He would know what to do about Dickens, about this stick. She wheeled lazily around.

Captain Kingsley's great paws were wrapped around Santiago's neck. Santiago gasped hoarsely; his legs kicked, but the polar bear was holding him at arm's length, so Santiago couldn't reach him.

The haze of pain cleared, and Penelope understood what was happening again. "No!" she thundered.

Captain Kingsley let go of Santiago, who fell limply into the water. Was he alive?

"No!" Penelope thundered again. First Dickens, and now Santiago—no, it had to stop. She focused her anger and despair and revenge into the slender harpoon, and hurled it toward the polar bear.

It struck Captain Kingsley full in the chest. He staggered, then locked his knees and stood unmoving, staring at Dickens on the beach.

Frenchie splashed to his friend's side. "Let me 'elp." He reached for the harpoon to pull it out, but it was too high. He leapt higher, but still couldn't reach it. Santiago was up and staggering toward them.

Suddenly, the polar bear keeled over. Frenchie tried to get out of the way, but Captain Kingsley's body fell half on top of him. He landed heavily. Both polar bear and penguin were knocked out.

Penelope looked down at her own broken shoulder. Then up at Santiago. She whispered, "Help."

20

"TELL STORIES."

Santiago carried Penelope to shore and laid her beside Dickens. He couldn't move Captain Kingsley, who still lay in the water with Frenchie half under him.

From the *Hallowe'en* came cries:

"Look! The Captain's hurt!"

"That's a sea monster. There's sure to be others about."

"Let's get out of here!"

The crew of the *Hallowe'en* didn't wait for their captain and first mate. Unhindered by those on shore, they raised anchor, unfurled sails and left.

Penelope was sure her life had just ended. But she didn't pass out; she didn't go to sleep. Instead, she just hurt. Slowly, her breathing eased, and she found she could sit up.

She stood on her three good legs and limped to Dickens. Blood covered the sand near him, but Santiago had removed the harpoon.

"Is he alive?"

"Barely," said Santiago in a deep, sad voice. He held a bunch of seaweed on the wound, stopping the bleeding.

Penelope nodded, sorrow filling her, too. She lay beside Dickens, holding seaweed to her own injury and watching the slow rise and fall of his chest. When her emotions eased off, she tried again to rise to help Santiago take care of things.

Penelope limped to the *Liberty*, where she was sunk in shallow water. Babying her injured foreleg, she finally climbed aboard. In the cabin, she found their medicine chest. She mixed sleeping powder into two cups of drinking water and brought them back to shore.

Together, Penelope and Santiago heaved the polar bear off the penguin. Captain Kingsley and Frenchie were still unconscious, so Santiago forced the sleeping potion down their throats. Sleeping would relieve the Captain's pains and keep Frenchie quiet until the Talberts could decide what to do with them. In fact, they'd have to stay drugged, or the pigs wouldn't be able to handle them.

Santiago and Penelope sat on the white sand by Dickens. He still breathed, but he wouldn't wake.

Santiago gently helped Penelope lie down to rest and lay close to her for comfort. "We fought," he whispered. "Against such evil, that's all you can do."

As dawn came, Santiago carried Dickens inland to a small, fresh-water spring and came back to support Penelope as she staggered weakly to the make-shrift nest. All day, they watched over Dickens. Santiago left only long enough to help the groggy Frenchie and Captain Kingsley stumble into the shade of the trees before giving them more sleeping potion. The Captain's injury was already healing, as was Penelope's.

Once during that day, Dickens' eyes fluttered, and Penelope thought he would awake. Instead he moaned, and then was quiet. Sometime in the afternoon, Santiago forced Penelope to eat some fruit. But mostly, she sat beside him and watched. By evening, when Dickens started to run a fever, they despaired.

Santiago went back to the *Liberty* again and found a packet of Chinese herbs that were supposed to help break a fever. Santiago brewed a tea, and Penelope spoon-fed it to Dickens. Then Penelope watched over him without sleeping herself. Every four hours, she fed him more medicinal tea while Santiago changed the seaweed on his wound.

Finally, at dawn on the third day, Dickens' eyes opened.

"Mother?" His whisper was as still as the ocean in the tropics.

"I'm here," Penelope reassured him. She wanted to weep at the word, mother. Dickens had never used it before.

"Are you okay?"

"I'm fine." Her own foreleg was still sore, but she hardly noticed it in her anguish over Dickens.

"Story. Tell stories," Dickens said.

So Penelope told stories of their sailing for a year and a day. And she had much to tell. She told of finding Dickens wrapped in Spanish moss, and how he cried and cried. She told of how sailing calmed him, so that they were always upon the high seas those first months. She told of his first steps, his first swim, his first word. She told of the black sand islands they had explored. She told of the songs of the humpback whales and swimming with the pod. She told of the ocean and the stars.

It was Dickens who finally whispered, "Shhh!"

Then he turned over and slept—without fever—and when he awoke, he was hungry.

They stayed on the island while everyone healed. They were careful to keep Frenchie and Captain Kingsley drugged the whole while. Santiago worked steadily on boat repairs, so that after ten days, he sailed alone back to St. George's. He found Captain Brice and brought Penelope back her journals and harp.

Captain Brice arrived herself in the *Endurance* a day later. She waded ashore carrying huge shackles. Her curly hair was escaping her captain's hat, as usual, and she was grinning widely. "Caught the villains, did you?"

Captain Brice and her crew loaded Captain Kingsley and Frenchie into her brig.

"Authorities have found the horrible collection on the *Hallowe'en*. There's a bounty out for their capture," Captain Brice said.

"Will you collect the bounty?" Penelope asked.

"Ah, no. That would be too easy a thing for Captain Kingsley. Instead, I'll keep them in my brig and keep them half-sedated while we sail around Cape Horn. Somewhere in the middle of the South Pacific, I'll find a deserted island and leave them there."

Penelope nodded. It was a fitting punishment.

Finally, everyone was well enough to climb on board the *Liberty*. The year and a day was almost over, and they didn't want to be late. They set sail for a distant bayou.

21

"MOTHER?"

Two weeks later, the evening tide carried them toward the dark waters of the bayou where they had found Dickens. While fog puddled over their boat, Penelope worried about Dickens' mother. Was she still alive? Would she come for Dickens? But Dickens sat beside her and sang sea shanties, and Penelope was captured afresh by his voice that held a hint of whale songs, of tides that rise and fall and sweet rains upon the waves. Slowly, her heart quieted.

They slept late, ate late. That afternoon, Santiago paced the deck, worrying, until Dickens paced right behind, imitating Santiago's every move. Finally, they both collapsed in laughter. Santiago pulled Dickens up, and they danced a jig around the mainsail while Penelope sang shanties.

By now, Dickens had grown so long and thick that he couldn't go below to their cabin.

At sunset, when the fog crept in again, Penelope and Santiago put on jackets and sat on deck with Dickens.

Once they were settled, Dickens asked Penelope, "Tell us stories of our year and a day."

And Penelope had much to tell. There were tales of joy about teaching Dickens to read, to sing, to fish, and to live among the intelligent creatures of the world with integrity and honesty.

It was Dickens who finally whispered, "Shhh! Something comes!"

Around the *Liberty*, the waters swelled, rocking the boat until the ship's bell donged gently.

Penelope hugged Dickens one last time. "Now. Go and meet your mother." Her heart was both full with the joy of living and empty from the joy of letting go. *How could it be both at the same time?* she wondered.

Dickens hesitated.

Santiago said quickly, "We're here."

Together, Santiago, Penelope and Dickens stood and faced the water.

Out of the fog, words came: "Where is the child?"

Penelope nudged Dickens.

He turned his head, trying to see through the fog. "Mother?"

From the murk, a narrow nose appeared, and then, a massive head followed by endless coils.

Dickens looked up and up and up. He squeaked, "Mother?"

"No. I'm your father."

Such a joyous reunion! Father and son cried, laughed, studied each other, and talked with voices that were almost identical, except that Dickens' was still high pitched.

Santiago put his foreleg around Penelope, and they watched with glad hearts.

At last, Dickens' father turned to them. "Thank you! You saved my son's life."

"Kind sir," Penelope asked, "where is Dickens' mother?"

"I know not. I only know that I lost her in the storm. I swam for months searching for her until one day, I heard a voice singing. It was Dickens. And I heard you telling him the story of how you found him."

Penelope understood now. When she had thought whales were making the waters swell, it had really been this sea serpent watching over his son.

"You were there," the sea serpent explained, "with that brute of a polar bear. When he threw the harpoon, it hit her. Here." He brushed his foreleg against his right chest. "I tilted the boat so you could escape. But then, she was gone."

Dickens touched the scar on his chest. His eyes never left his father's face.

"She knew," Penelope whispered. "She couldn't survive, and she had to send Dickens out on the waters of the ocean, so you would find him."

"I wanted to claim him much earlier, but I didn't know if I could trust you. I had to wait, so you would lead me back here. I hoped to find my wife." The sea serpent bent his head and nuzzled Dickens. "You look like your mother. She had a green hide, too."

And now they noticed that the father sea serpent was mostly brown. If you judged by his father's size, Dickens was barely a third grown.

Dickens said, "Tell me stories about my mother."

And there was much to tell of the love between two sea serpents and their hopes for their child.

From the *Liberty*, the Talberts watched in wonder. Penelope wrote her first sea shanty about creatures seeking for a home. Santiago took out his most recent map and decorated it with monstrous coils. Finally, they strung hammocks, so they could keep watching the family reunion, and eventually, they slept beneath the stars. Dickens, for the first time in his life, slept safely tucked inside the coil of his father's tail.

The next day, the sea serpents and the pigs had a conference.

"Where can I go and safely raise my son?" asked Dickens' father.

Penelope pulled out a sea chart Santiago had drawn. Santiago nodded and tapped it.

Penelope said, "We've found an island where you can be safe."

"The Black Sand Island?" Dickens asked. "Oh, father, you'll love it there."

"Will you come with us?" asked Dickens' father. "You can come for a visit, or maybe it will be a safe place for you, a place you'll want to stay."

"Yes," Penelope and Santiago said together. And Dickens hugged Penelope until she squealed with joy.

Penelope and Santiago set sail that day, with Dickens and his father swimming along beside them. By now, Dickens was swimming most of the time and only came on deck at evening to sing and visit.

The *Liberty*, followed by two sea serpents, sailed back to the Atlantic and down to the south Caribbean. At long last, they came home to a harbor of a green island with black sand. The evening tide pushed their sailboat far up a river, where Penelope and Santiago tied up.

"Look!" Dickens cried.

A broad marsh—with lots of black mud—spread out before them.

"Home!" Penelope said happily.

Santiago agreed. "Home."

Later that year, Penelope gave birth to a litter of black and white piglets. She named the first-born, Victoria Marie. Cricket visited soon after in the *Mercator*, and agreed to be the piglets' god-mother.

So it was that Penelope and Santiago Talbert spent their days beachcombing with sea serpents who quoted poetry. And dancing jigs in the mud with their piglets. And singing, singing, singing, shanties of the seas.

ABOUT THE AUTHOR

Award-winning children's book author **DARCY PATTISON** has received starred reviews from *PW*, *Kirkus*, and *BCCB*. Her title, *The Journey of Oliver K. Woodman* received an Irma Black Picture Book Honor award. Twice her books have been named NSTA Outstanding Science Trade Books. Known for her Novel Revision Workshop, she has helped shepherd many debut novels.

Her novels include stories of troubled families, fantasy worlds, and aliens shipwrecked on Earth. "Compelling and . . .hopeful," critics say of ***Saucy and Bubba*** is a contemporary retelling of Hansel and Gretel. ***The Girl, the Gypsy, and the Gargoyle*** leads fantasy readers into a hidden world where miracles redeem mistakes. ***Vagabonds*** leads fantasy readers into a stone world where everything is twisted and backwards. She is the 2007 recipient of the Arkansas Governor's Arts Award for Individual Artist for her contributions to children's literature.

NEWSLETTER

For more information on Darcy Pattison's books, sign up for her VIP Mailing List here:

http://mimshouse.com/newsletter

CPSIA information can be obtained
at www.ICGtesting.com
Printed in the USA
FFOW04n1026040416
22890FF

9 781629 440651